DIALOGUE WITH AN ANGEL

Fred Hermesmann

To Susan

Fred Hermesmann

ATHENA PRESS
LONDON

ISBN 1 932077 78 2

First Published 2004 by
ATHENA PRESS
Queen's House, 2 Holly Road
Twickenham TW1 4EG
United Kingdom

Printed for Athena Press

DIALOGUE WITH AN ANGEL

I wish to dedicate this book to all married couples in the world, to my own family and especially to my wife Lorraine, whom I always consider the soul of our family

Acknowledgements

I wish to acknowledge Father Michael Martell O.S.A. (Order of St. Augustine), and Father Allan Charnon O.S.A., who expressed in their homilies many of the ideas discussed in this dialogue; my brother Hans Georg Hermesmann, who had a great influence on this project, and, of course, my friend Ray Decloux who reviewed the book many times and encouraged me always to carry on.

Contents

Preface

Each and every one of our human family will be faced with the same fundamental question in his or her life at one time or another. This question relates to the relationship with God. While it is impossible for each of us to comprehend God, we still can establish this relationship with God if we understand what God really wants from us.

It is not too difficult to see the will of God, if we use as the basis of our understanding the fact that GOD IS LOVE. Once we have grasped this basic fundamental principle, our life will change, our relationship to our fellow human beings will change and we can face the problems in our daily life much easier; ultimately our life can be happier.

This booklet is not intended to be a theological thesis. It is meant to be thought-provoking, covering difficult questions with the help of a relatively easily understood story. It is intended as a tool for meditation and prayer.

It is a story where questions which we hear quite often from non-believers are discussed, but these are also questions with which we too have to wrestle very often. The story is written to relate to the reader the fundamental message of God's love without a lecturing style. It is supposed to be a joy to read and, as in all good stories, the ending is a happy one.

Harry and Beatrice, a Marriage in Our Times

Harry M., a very successful businessman living in Vancouver, was ready to make one of the most important decisions in his life. Looking out of his office window on this glorious sunny day in the early spring, he felt proud to be able to experience the beauty of his chosen city, a city where mountains and ocean meet right at the doorstep of its boundary.

Vancouver is at its finest in late March or early April. On some days the sun may shine in a cloudless sky. A gentle wind from the southwest may bring fresh air from the ocean and blow away the pollution generated every day by the traffic-congested city. The snow-covered mountains, rising to a level of 1800 meters from the ocean on the north side of the city, present a postcard-magnificent picture.

The rains in the winter and early spring convert to snow at higher levels. It is not unusual that the top of the surrounding mountains are covered with meter-deep snow while the city below is engulfed in the colors of its gardens, parks and trees. There is no other major city north of Vancouver. The mountains make this impossible.

Only one road goes north along the shores of Howe Sound, a fjord reaching a length of about fifty kilometers. The road has many curves and corners dictated by the ocean on the west side and by the mountains on the east side. It is treacherous and dangerous to drive on this road not because of the oncoming traffic but because of the possibility of fallen rocks or landslides. This road is magnificent in its setting. It leads to the Whistler and Blackcomb mountain resorts, two of the top ski resorts in the world. On a clear day on top of the Peak or Seventh Heaven chairlifts, skiers can simply rest a few minutes and stand in awe to take in more fully the view of the snow-covered mountains surrounding the resorts.

Harry loved Vancouver. This clear and sunny day in early

spring justified his decision, made years ago, to move to the city he had fallen in love with. It was not a normal, average day in the life of Vancouver. It was one of those grandiose, maybe 'ultimate days', which gave Harry a feeling of greatness, and also the arrogance of a person who thought himself to be better than others.

Harry loved the ultimate. He was a stock promoter and trader in shares who not only worked for the interest of his clients, but also for his own benefit. People in his office thought him to be pompous, overbearing and self-promoting. He annoyed people with his constant boasting of how smart he was in his investment decisions.

Harry was obsessed with making money, and the bull market of the Nineties provided him with many opportunities to further his cause. Years ago he had seen a film about stock manipulations on Wall Street in which his hero proclaimed that greed was good, that greed was the main driving force to create wealth. So whenever Harry made a killing in his stock manipulations, he justified his actions with the statement: 'Greed is good.'

Harry had some spectacular successes for a few years. Luck was with him and he made some intelligent stock calls, especially in a major gold mining swindle in 1997. In late 1996 when the stock was at the highest level, he had a feeling that he should get in on the frenzy, but instead of buying the stock, he had sold a large number of shares short. He purchased the shares, which he had sold short, at a fraction of the sales price when it was discovered that there was no 'gold in them thar hills'. What was termed as the largest gold find in the world turned into the biggest mining fiasco ever. The profit earned on this deal was simply huge.

These and other windfalls gave him the feeling of being invincible. Years of saving money allowed him the financial freedom he so longed for, but also the arrogance of a 'know-it-all' attitude. Harry was not particularly liked because of this attitude. People looked with envy at his successes and secretly wished his luck would change, but he did not give them this pleasure. He carried on and only complained about the taxes he had to pay. In reality he did not pay the taxes which were due to be paid resulting from earning large profits. He had hired consultants and lawyers who had advised him on how to avoid paying taxes by transferring large amounts into offshore investments and how to set up bogus companies in Caribbean islands which would handle all stock transactions.

Harry felt on top of the world this beautiful spring morning. He had decided to accept an invitation to a party given to a select group of wealthy people in Whistler by a brokerage house promoting investment in Caribbean islands or other tax havens. He thought that it would be a good idea to have his eggs in more than one basket. This party was promoted with all the trimmings: free food, free lodging, free entertainment, female company if he so wished, a taste of the real good life – a party which was right according to his status as a wealthy individual.

This invitation also came at the right time for him because it gave him the reason to escape the dullness and dreariness of his married life. He was happy to accept. Secretly he wanted to find out how he could divorce his wife Beatrice, and hide his wealth, so that in case of a divorce he would not have to share the money he had earned with a wife he did not love anymore.

Harry and Beatrice had been married for fifteen years. They had met in Montreal while he had attended Loyola University. When they met she was a beautiful, shy woman. He was attracted to this shyness because it gave her an aura of being secret and distant, a distance which he, a brash, self-assured, know-it-all student of a Jesuit-influenced University, found interesting and alluring. They had met at the Montreal airport during the early fall on a rainy evening. Beatrice, while intrigued by Harry's energy, ego and desire to achieve, was initially hesitant to start a relationship with him. She wanted to pursue her own career as a teacher. Her wish was to teach young children, maybe those with learning difficulties.

Beatrice felt that this would provide her with a sense of purpose in her life, in doing something good for someone who had less, especially someone who was not fully appreciated, or who had not realized his or her full potential in society. Now after fifteen years of marriage she found that she had made a mistake. She could not combine her calling to teach the underprivileged with the desire of her husband to be successful in his business dealings at all costs.

Harry's feelings for Beatrice had also cooled. In the first years of their marriage, they both were passionately in love with each other. Their friends and relatives had congratulated them many times that they were such a good match. They congratulated Harry because he had made such a wise choice in Beatrice, a beautiful and intelligent woman, and they congratulated Beatrice because she had married a successful, self-assured businessman with a great future who would be able to provide her with an appropriate lifestyle.

Beatrice and Harry were married in Montreal, but had moved to Vancouver two years later, when it was apparent that better opportunities for success were on the West Coast. Besides, they liked skiing and tennis. What better place to tend to these sporting desires than in Vancouver?

Harry and Beatrice had three children. The first two were twins born in Vancouver, a boy and a girl who were very close to each other and seldom let anyone, especially their younger brother, a slightly mentally challenged boy, interfere with their relationship. Charles, the third child, felt therefore like an outcast. He was eight years old and was neither accepted by the twins nor by his father, who had never wanted another child after the twins. In fact he had asked Beatrice to get an abortion, but she had refused. Since then, their marriage had turned into a battleground of wills, and the atmosphere between both Beatrice and Harry had become more and more poisonous. These were not great battles, like explosions of passionate statements, with arguments and abusive behavior, but a steady flow of little insults and derogatory remarks, against which Beatrice had little defense.

She wished to have the opportunity to have intelligent discussions about the problem in their marriage, but Harry would build a wall around himself, bury himself in financial reports of companies in which he wanted to invest. He reminded Beatrice almost daily of the fact that she had a good life, that he provided her with money and that she should count herself lucky to have such a good and wonderful husband as a provider. He neglected to tell her that he had one or two affairs during the last three years and that he had slowly tried to develop a plan on how to terminate the marriage in the least costly way. He simply did not feel it to be reasonable to have to share the wealth he, through wise investment strategies, had accumulated in the last ten years.

Harry came from a Catholic family. Under the control of his rather strong-willed mother, he had attended a Catholic school, learned his catechism, and after twelve years of schooling graduated from a Catholic school in Montreal in order to attend Loyola University. He did not have a great passion for his faith; in fact he was riddled with doubts. After many discussions with his university professors, he eventually concluded that God did not exist, and that if he did, he must have been a loser. He had drifted into other religions but realized that these were not much different; he especially criticized the hypocrisy attached to many faiths and used these arguments as an excuse to put his interest in other affairs, especially the pursuit of making money. Money for him had the only true value, a value which he could touch, a value over which he had control and a value which he did not, in particular, want to share with anyone else.

Beatrice for her part did not realize this obsession initially. She was a gullible woman, beautiful, sensitive and influenced by the many things money could buy. Of course Harry showered her with expensive gifts. The diamond ring for their engagement, for example, was a showpiece, admired by many. Years later she would regret this gullibility and she began to grow more and more bitter, especially when she was faced with the lack of real communication between herself and her husband. She would be irritated by the little day-to-day occurrences which, if overexposed, could result in serious problems for both.

For example, Harry would not share in the household chores. Beatrice would complain about that. He would use that complaint as an opportunity to get his point across, his point being that household chores were really women's work and therefore *hers* and not *his*. His function was to provide her with a good lifestyle. She should be really grateful for that. His standard phrase was that the least he could expect from her was a little understanding for the difficult tasks he had to face day in day out to make such a lifestyle possible.

These battles went on and on. Sometimes each of them thought that he or she had won a little skirmish, but that steady dose of daily poison made their life miserable. Charles could sense these tensions between Harry and Beatrice, but due to his inability to express his feelings well, he suffered the most. He loved his parents in his own way, trying to smile, trying to work hard on his homework and trying to impress his parents with truisms, which his more intelligent brother and sister would simply accept as a given. He would get upset when they took away his toys, especially his little teddy bear, the only real friend he thought he had. He would cry hysterically when they took it from him to toss it to each other. He would run between them trying to catch the teddy bear, but could never do it because his brother and sister were too fast. It was not a happy life for him and his mother, who tried to protect him from the other children and the impatience of his father, Harry.

Beatrice felt more and more helpless, especially when Harry indicated – which was often – that they would not have had all this trouble if she had only consented to an abortion. Further, during the last few years, the word 'love' had disappeared from their day-to-day vocabulary. Instead, the words 'You should have done this and that' or 'Why did you do this and that?' made up a daily dose of the sporadic conversation Beatrice and Harry managed to come up with. While Beatrice tried to the best of her ability to salvage some kind of common ground, Harry was always evasive and immediately put a wall around himself. He felt that any attempt to break this wall was an attempt to enter his private life.

Harry, for his part, was not a bad guy. He provided well for his family and was able to guarantee a good upper middle-class lifestyle which was necessary to maintain his status in the community where they lived. Harry was self-assured and self-appreciating. He always said to himself, 'I do so many things for my family, but I do not get the appreciation I deserve at home. And besides, Beatrice has not been able to adapt to the demands of the lifestyle a man of my status and wealth should be accustomed to. Beatrice lives in a mindset of fifteen years ago, when yes there was some kind of romantic love, a love long forgotten.'

All these and other thoughts were on Harry's mind when he set out on this beautiful spring day to visit his consultants and their entourage in Whistler. He was ready to live it up and make a final decision about the divorce as soon as he was back home the next morning.

Since Harry loved the 'ultimate', he naturally drove the 'ultimate driving machine' – a BMW – thought of as a status symbol for many successful investors. Off he went to Whistler, in order to negotiate another tax saving deal with his consultants.

The Incident

Every traveler who drives on the road to Whistler will be greeted at the entrance to the road with a warning sign. Usually in late March, the sign reads: 'Watch for falling rocks.' Harry saw the sign but did not, as most of the other drivers do, pay much attention to it. Listening to his favorite talk show this late afternoon, he locked the car into cruise control at a little above the speed limit. The sun was shining from the west, barely above the horizon, and his sunroof was open. The wind and the fresh air tingled the top of his head. Harry was happy because he had finally made up his mind to end his marriage. He would probably come to a settlement which would allow Beatrice a reasonable lifestyle. Since he had most of his assets hidden from her, just as much as he had them hidden from the government, he felt safe and sound. He thought that he was a reasonable man, a man who, even though he did not love his wife anymore, could guarantee a good life for her and the children.

Deep in thought, he carried on driving. He was surprised that the traffic was relatively light. There were not many cars on the road – in fact, none, except one which was traveling approximately one or two kilometers behind him. Also, the traffic on the other side was very light. He had not seen any cars or trucks on the southbound side of the road for quite a while. He was expecting a delay further north on the road due to maintenance or construction work.

He came around one of the corners and was confronted with an unusual sight, the sight of a motorcycle driver who obviously had no idea about how to drive the heavy machine. Not only was he driving way below the speed limit, but he was driving the machine like a person who had never taken a lesson. He moved from one side to the other, jerking the engine up and then down, slowing it to 5 kph and then speeding it up to more than 35 kph.

'This is an unusual sight,' said Harry, laughing to himself.

17

'Here is a Hell's Angel who doesn't know how to control a Harley Davidson. This has to be something new for these beer-belly, tattooed bastards! This guy seems to have just graduated in learning how to drive a horse drawn carriage, never mind a heavy motorcycle.'

After watching the driver in front of him for a short while and having slowed down his car to a near crawl, he finally became impatient. He said to himself, 'I have to pass this idiot! I can't drive behind this joker and wait until the next passing line. I have no time; I must be in Whistler in one hour. I am late already!'

With this in mind, he closed the gap between him and the motorcycle driver who was still twisting and turning on the road ahead of him. The road was very narrow and the yellow double line indicated that the passing of any vehicle was forbidden and dangerous. Harry disobeyed these road signs and drove the car across the double yellow line in order to pass. While passing, the motorcycle driver made a final twist to the left side, almost hitting Harry's car. Harry was able to avoid the driver with a swift turn to the left, bringing the car completely into the southbound lane.

The motorcycle driver, upon realizing that a car was passing, immediately turned the machine toward the right-hand side of the road to avoid a serious accident. This meant, of course, that he would direct the machine towards the mountain side. Luckily he was able to slow the machine down and turn it around back to the northbound lane. A possible disaster had been narrowly avoided.

Harry, in his impatience, was not so lucky. He was able to avoid hitting the motorcycle driver, but by putting all his attention to the scene in front of him, he didn't see the upcoming sharp turn of the road to the right. At the last moment he was able to wheel the car to the right side of the road. He looked in the mirror to see what had happened to the motorcycle driver. As a result he didn't see the rock in the northbound lane. The rock had to be the size of a football; it was not round but had sharp edges. It was lying close to the middle of the road, bordering the yellow double line.

Like a magnet, Harry's car was drawn to the rock. The rock hit the front tire of the car and the force of the speed with which Harry was driving resulted in a blowout. The best tire in the world, even the one which was installed on his 'ultimate driving machine', could not withstand this force. It made a deep cut on the inside of the tire. Harry almost lost control over the car because of this force. He immediately reduced his speed and was lucky. If he had hit the rock at 80 kph, he would have lost control over his vehicle. But only traveling at about 40 kph, he managed to keep control and steer the car to a nearby lookout on the west side of the road. He made a left turn to this lookout and limped over to this safer place to park.

Full of anger, Harry stumbled out of his car and had a closer look at the tire to see whether the damage was very serious or not. What he saw made him more furious. The first barrage of swearing was directed at the government, which, despite all the taxes being paid by its citizens, was unable to maintain a safe road. Of course, he overlooked the fact that he himself paid very few taxes. The next barrage was directed towards that stupid motorcycle rider. If this driver had only known how to drive his machine, he, Harry, would have been able to keep all his attention on the road. Then, he surely would have then been able to avoid hitting the rock.

Harry was just about to open the trunk and pick up the tools to change the wheel when he heard the roaring noise of a motorcycle. He looked up and saw the motorcycle driver he had met on the road approaching him and slowing down the machine. The driver stopped and, not knowing how to park the motorcycle, leaned the machine against a nearby tree.

Some Hell's Angel you are, thought Harry. *Not only do you not know how to drive a motorcycle, you don't even know how to park it! I think I must have a serious talk with these guys and tell them that they definitely will have an image problem if they admit people who don't even understand the basic rudiments of operating a motorcycle.*

Harry also had another reaction: *fear*. Deep down he realized that he could have been responsible for a serious accident. He could have injured or even killed this man. He was prepared for a confrontation as he searched for a wrench which he could use to defend himself. He prepared himself for the worst.

While he was looking for a wrench, the driver approached Harry from behind and stood very close to him while he was bent over searching in the trunk. 'Howdy,' said the driver and tipped his finger on his helmet. 'Having a good day?'

The driver was a strong man, about two meters tall and 250 lb heavy. He appeared to be like the stereotypic Hell's Angel, all muscle, beer belly, chains, rings and leather outfit. He had a thick beard, which covered most of his face. He looked rather fearsome.

Harry was prepared for a fight. He had just found the wrench; made of hardened steel, about three feet long, it was a weapon to be reckoned with. He now could defend himself, if necessary. He was a bit of a coward and abhorred fist fights, but like a rat when cornered, would not give up easily. Harry turned around to face his enemy. Standing there with the wrench in his right hand, he immediately started to argue with the driver.

'This was all your fault! You drive like a cowboy. You drive like you own the road. You have no regard for your fellow drivers, who at least have to pass a driving test to get on the road. I bet you don't even have a license!' he exclaimed.

The man replied, 'Not so fast, my friend. I prevented you from having a far more serious accident. I helped you slow down. If you had come around the corner a few seconds sooner, the rock which was lying on the road would have fallen through the open space in your sunroof and would have hit you right on the head. The least you could do is say "thank you".'

'How do you know this? Are you some kind of magician or fortuneteller?' asked Harry.

'No,' replied the man. 'I am your guardian angel, who wants to have a word with you.'

'What do you mean, my *guardian angel*? As far as I am concerned, you are a Hell's Angel, and I doubt that the devil employs guardian angels!' exclaimed Harry.

'Why do think I am a Hell's Angel? Just because I have a beer belly and a beard, drive a Harley Davidson and look a little dirty and musty, must I be a Hell's Angel? You must correct your vision a little bit, because your vision may lead you to assumptions from which you draw the wrong conclusions. Not every beer-bellied driver of a Harley Davidson motorcycle is a Hell's Angel,' said the angel dryly.

'But you are wearing the rings, the helmet and also the leather jacket, which are the status symbols of Hell's Angels,' answered Harry with a few doubts in his mind, his confidence shaken. 'Even on your jacket you have imprinted the words "Hell's Angel". I saw them while driving behind you on this cursed road!'

The angel replied, 'Have a closer look! Yes, you can see *Angel* and yes, you can see a capital "H" and an "e" following it, but it clearly says on the jacket "Heaven's Angel". You should get your vision checked – and in fact, that is why I was sent here. I was sent here to *improve* your vision so that you can differentiate more clearly between what is important in your life and what is not.'

'There is nothing wrong with my vision!' replied Harry angrily. 'I know very well what I should focus on in life. I am a very successful businessman, envied by many for my success. I don't have to improve my vision or understanding about what is important and what is not. For me, success is money, and the more I have, the happier I am.'

'You seemed to be quite sure about the value of your money,' said the angel. 'I am not. Money has no value in itself. It is simply an instrument for transferring value from one person to another. In other words it makes the exchange of goods and services easier. If you, therefore, at the end of your life, sit on a pot full of gold or have a big bank account, that amount of money is absolutely useless to you, especially when you have it hidden away in a few obscure bank accounts in the Caribbean…'

'How do you know about that?' answered Harry suspiciously. 'Are you sure that you're an angel and not from the tax department?'

He thought, *I had better be more careful about what I say from now on… Somehow I have to get rid of this guy. He is definitely getting on my nerves!*

Loudly he said, 'Listen, man, I have to get on with my trip. Because of your stupid behavior on the road, I have a flat tire which I have to fix. I have no more time for idle talk about vision. I have an appointment in Whistler. It's very important that I be there on time. I suggest that you carry on with your travels and I also suggest that you work on your driving skills. Maybe you should visit a driving school. They could teach you a few things about driving a motorcycle like a real Hell's Angel, not like a guy who has barely graduated to be in control of a horse drawn carriage.'

'Funny that you should say this,' replied the angel. 'I used to drive a chariot in my days as a soldier in the Roman army. I guess because of that expertise, I was asked to try this Harley Davidson. Sorry I couldn't control this machine better. Even as an angel, you never stop learning.

'But to prove that I am who I say I am,' continued the angel, 'I will fix your tire in no time at all. You see, I can work miracles – and where I come from, time is not of the essence. Time as you know it does not exist there.'

After a moment's silence, the angel asked, 'Do you have a watch?'

Harry looked in astonishment at his watch and said, 'Yes, of course, it is one of my Rolexes. I like to wear a different brand of expensive Swiss-made watches every day of the week. Today is Rolex day. In fact it is exactly 4:55 P.M.'

Harry thought to himself, *If this guy is for real, than I should give him a try and let him prove himself.* Aloud he continued, 'You say you can fix this tire in no time flat? I believe that this tire because of its deep cut on the inside isn't even fixable. But I'll give you a chance to work a miracle. Prove to me that you are an angel and fix this tire in no time!'

'Okay!' said the angel. 'But there is a condition attached to it.'

'And what is that?'

'The condition is that we have a little chat about what is important in your life, so that your vision about what the "real ultimate" is in your life can be improved.'

'I have no time for long discussions. I want to get going and I need the tire fixed. You can fix the tire, but no long discussions about some spiritual stuff which I don't even care about anyway,' said Harry.

The angel replied, 'I guarantee you personally that you will not lose any time with me when we have our discussion because we will be in a timeless environment. Therefore, if you wish, you can carry on with your trip after our dialogue and still be on time with your tax consultants in Whistler. In fact I will *save* you time! Your tire can be fixed with a touch. You don't even have to remove the wheel.'

'Well,' said Harry reluctantly, 'let's get going, then. You fix the tire and I will agree to a talk. But before I agree, I suggest you tell me a little bit more about yourself. Who are you really?'

The angel said, 'Thank you, Harry, you are great. You have really helped me by agreeing to have this dialogue. I will tell you now who I am and the reason why we met. Please listen to my story. I will try to make it as brief as possible.'

The Angel and his Story

After a brief moment the angel said, 'As I told you before, during my life on earth, I was a Roman soldier. My name was Longinus. I was a common soldier in the Roman army. My father was also in the army and after retirement was allotted by the emperor a large plot of land in southern Italy. My father was a good businessman and developed an interest for horse breeding. We bred horses for the army. When I became of age, I was drawn into the army and was assigned to ride horses, or drive chariots when required.'

The angel continued, 'The chariot drivers were in big demand because the army required mobility in the occupied countries. Trouble spots were all over the place and one of the most volatile and troublesome areas was the land of the Jews. As you can see, nothing has changed in two thousand years. The Jews were a stubborn lot and one of the most ruthless procurators was assigned to this part of the world to subdue the Jews. His name was Pontius Pilate.'

'You mean Pontius Pilate, the man who judged Jesus?' asked Harry.

'Yes, the same Pontius Pilate,' answered the angel. 'In fact, Pontius Pilate was my superior, and I was present at the trial of Jesus. Would you like to hear about the proceedings of this trial?'

Harry said, 'Yes, that would be interesting.'

The angel said, 'I was one of the soldiers who flogged Jesus, put a crown of thorns on his head and finally crucified him after a few hours of torment. I was also the one who ensured that he was dead by spearing him with my lance.'

'So you are a witness of the crucifixion!' exclaimed Harry. 'That is very interesting. I always thought that the story of the crucifixion was an overblown event, touched up by two thousand years of Christian heritage and tradition with hardly any relevance to our current times.'

He paused and said sententiously, 'You must know that I used to belong to the Roman Catholic Church, but I left because I couldn't attach any importance to the crucifixion of Jesus Christ. I always believed that the constant reminder of the crucifixion was to serve only one purpose, that is, to make the faithful feel guilty about the death of Jesus on the cross, which of course is a good tool for the priests with which to exercise control. Yes, it would be a good idea to hear from a witness who participated in the crucifixion. I would like to know what really happened.'

'Do you want a vivid description of the crucifixion?' asked the angel.

'Yes, that would be great,' said Harry. 'I really would like to know what went on and how you soldiers punished the victim. This would provide me with a more balanced view, a view without sentimentalities based on Christian tradition. I am very interested to get a true picture.'

'You will get your wish,' answered the angel. 'I will briefly describe the trial and execution of Jesus. We will use this description of the trial as the starting point of our dialogue, the real reason why we have met.'

The angel continued; 'It was early in the morning on the last day of the week, the day before one of the Jews' most holy days, the Passover Feast, the feast where the Jewish people celebrate their freedom from the Egyptian slavery. They commemorate on this day the events of 1500 years prior, when their ancestors were guided out of Egypt by their leader Moses to the Promised Land. On this day Pontius Pilate was asked to judge a man called Jesus, a man who the Jews said had proclaimed himself to be the Messiah, blaspheming their God and making himself an equal of their God. Pontius Pilate was very reluctant to judge Jesus and hand him over to be crucified. Therefore he first handed him over to us soldiers for a whipping and to have a little fun with him. He thought that this was punishment enough for a man who blasphemed a God about which he knew very little.'

'How did you flog Jesus?' asked Harry, full of interest.

'We hit Jesus with whips which had a piece of metal attached to the end of the rope,' said the angel. 'It was common practice in the Roman army to flog troublemakers this way. It was a very cruel punishment. Whenever you whipped a culprit, the metal piece on the end of the rope would cut a piece of flesh out of the body. The victim's body would be bloody in a short time, full of sores, and of course weakened. We hit Jesus about fifteen times. This ensured that he would survive the blows.

'Jesus was a strongly built man, about two meters tall,' continued the angel after a brief moment of silence. 'We whipped him very hard. Everyone had a turn. He was defenseless and, looking back, it gave us great pleasure to hit this defenseless human being. You know, when you are in power and in control and you are trained to exercise this power by all available means, pity does not come into play. The lust to see the blood of the unfortunate victim is the driving force. We flogged Jesus very hard and he lost a lot of blood and physical strength.'

'Is this the reason why Jesus was too weak and needed help to carry his cross to the place of execution?' asked Harry.

'Yes, that is possible,' replied the angel. 'Over and above the flogging, we made a crown of thorns and stuck it on his head. This in fact was my idea. I thought that this man was a revolutionary who had attacked the authority of the Roman emperor by proclaiming a kingship based on an authority higher than the one of the Roman emperor. I thought a fitting crown to ridicule that kingship should be a crown of thorns.

'When I placed that crown on the head of Jesus, I pricked my finger. It hurt badly, and out of anger I pushed the crown of thorns, which we had just made, even harder on his head. Jesus bled instantly. It must have been very painful but he stood there patiently and in silence. He looked me in the eyes, not accusingly, but more like a person who pitied me because of my lack of understanding of his mission and what he wanted to achieve.

'In fact,' the angel carried on, 'Jesus was not at all meek. He definitely never pleaded for mercy. He was more like a man with a mind set full of determination to carry out at all costs a mission – the mission, as I understood it later, to prove that love is stronger than all the evil in the world.'

The angel stopped for a moment and lowered his eyes in thoughtful silence. He then said, 'I believe that Jesus was very much in control of the trial because he knew what would happen in advance. He went freely to Jerusalem and fulfilled the mission of his life, which was his sacrifice on the cross. Nothing could stop him on that.'

'What happened after the whipping and the insults?' asked Harry.

The angel replied, 'Pontius Pilate asked Jesus again where he came from and Jesus said that if he, Pontius Pilate, would know the truth, he would recognize his nature and what he stood for. But in his present mindset, it would be impossible for him to comprehend the truth. Pontius Pilate was not used to this kind of language, especially not from someone whom he could, with a sign of his hand, condemn to death. Defensively, he asked, "What is truth?" – implying that truth does not exist.

'We will start our dialogue exactly where Pontius Pilate left off. We will start with the question of what is truth and how we can discover it in our life.'

'That would be a feat,' Harry replied. 'The only truth I am aware of is the value of money.'

'Well, we can discuss the value of money later,' said the angel, not very pleased. 'Let us carry on with my story. In order to continue, I have to tell you a little more about the crucifixion. We crucified three people that day, two murderers – rough-looking characters – with Jesus in the middle. You must realize that crucifixion is one of the most cruel death penalties ever invented. It is a slow death, which may last for hours or even days. The Roman authorities devised this form of death penalty as an example of what would happen to those people who challenged the authority of the Roman emperor and challenged the power of Rome itself. The victim is nailed on the cross. The nails are hammered through each wrist and through the feet. Not only is this very painful because the wrist is one of the main nerve centers in the body, but the victim suffocates very slowly. His lungs will collapse over a period of time.'

Harry asked, 'If this is the case, then why do crucifixes in the churches and on paintings show that the nails were driven through the hands?'

'I guess,' the angel answered, 'the artists years later who created these paintings and the crucifixes did not have a detailed knowledge about the methods used by the Romans. Remember, those artistic works were only created many years later, and what was written in the bible about the crucifixion was used as the source material to create those works of art. If Jesus had been nailed to the cross with nails hammered through his hands, the hands would not have been strong enough to support his body hanging on the cross.

'In any case,' the angel continued, 'the body of Jesus was weakened through the flogging. He died after a few hours on the cross, while the murderers who were crucified at his side were still alive. We soldiers were asked to make sure that the victims were dead so that the bodies could be removed from the crosses. We broke the leg bones of the murderers to make sure that they were dead. Jesus, because of his weakened condition, was dead already. I made sure of it by piercing his side with my lance.'

The angel carried on, deep in thought, 'Later on, many people said after his resurrection that Jesus was not really dead, that he could not have been dead because he was only a few hours on the cross. I am a witness of his death, because I am the soldier who pierced him with my lance.'

Harry asked, 'What was your general impression of Jesus when you met him at this most crucial hour at the trial? Was he meek? Was he defiant of the authorities? Was he revengeful to those who had delivered him to the Roman authorities? What do you think his attitude was towards the events which surrounded him?'

The angel replied, 'I died as a Roman soldier a few years later, fighting the Jewish people, at a time when Titus destroyed Jerusalem. I met Jesus as he really is, as the savior and redeemer of humanity. I talked to him about the events which led to his crucifixion and suddenly my eyes were opened. Suddenly I understood the reasons why all these events had to take place. I naturally felt very sorry about my participation in his crucifixion. But Jesus himself forgave me, as he will forgive everybody who does not understand the mystery of God and who is blinded by the wrong vision about what is true and what is not.'

'You mean you met Jesus later in the next life?' Harry asked. 'You have to be kidding me! I always thought that those people who killed Jesus were the first ones to go to hell, if hell exists. To me, those soldiers who participated in the crucifixion had a free pass to hell!'

The angel answered, 'Don't be too hasty in your judgment about what God should do and what God should not do. Leave your human judgment and understanding of God's wisdom at home. It is time that we improve your vision about your faith in a God who thinks and acts as God, and who is not a God whose actions have to be justified with human reasoning.'

The angel continued, 'When you see the face of Jesus as imprinted on the "shroud", for example, do you see the face of a vengeful man? Do you see the face of a loser? No, you see the face of a man, tired and overcome by pain, but also the face of a victorious man, serene and full of patience and love. It is a face which expresses the pride of having accomplished a great feat, a deed which is unique in the history of mankind. It is a face which expresses compassion with his tormentors and in fact with all humans, a face expressing to all humanity the words: "Father forgive them, they do not know what they do."'

Harry said thoughtfully, 'This is very well spoken. I think we should have the discussion you wanted to have with me. I am quite interested in what else you have to say. But be prepared for resistance. I'm not going to be easily convinced to change my way of life and what I believe to be true.'

'I am prepared to do that,' replied the angel. 'We should make a short agreement: I will fix this blasted tire on your "ultimate driving machine" and you will agree to a constructive dialogue. Maybe we should discuss this agreement in more detail.'

'Good idea,' said Harry.

The Agreement

Harry and the angel proceeded to a small bench which stood at the lookout. The sun was hidden partly behind a few clouds. It was an awe-inspiring view, which seemed to reveal some of the mysteries of the power of God.

The view to the west of the lookout on the road to Whistler can be quite beautiful in early spring, especially on a clear, early evening. Anybody who has experienced the early sunset in spring with the sun appearing as a yellow ball of fire can be inspired to enjoy with awe the beauty of creation. It usually takes ten to fifteen minutes to see the sun go down behind the mountainous islands located to the west of the lookout. It was exactly this scene where Harry and the angel agreed to the dialogue.

Harry, still doubtful but engulfed by the view of the sunset, said to the angel, 'Please promise me that this dialogue won't take too much time, and please fix my tire as soon as possible.'

'Why don't you take a look?' answered the angel. 'Do you see a flat tire?'

Harry turned around, and sure enough the tire was fixed. Harry was impressed. He said, 'You have a deal. Just give me a summary of what you want to talk about. But please, no sentimental stuff where I have to fall on my knees. I haven't done this lately and I don't want to start with this practice any time soon!'

The angel smiled and said to Harry, 'You remind me of a dried up cactus – dried up spiritually, that is – a cactus which grows in a desert and which longs for a little bit of water, a sign of life.'

'What do you mean comparing me to a dried up cactus?' asked Harry, angry at the comparison. 'I find this insulting! I am a successful businessman, reasonably intelligent, trained by the Jesuits of Loyola University in Montreal to think logically. I have applied this way of thinking very successfully to my various business endeavors. And now you compare me to a dried up desert cactus? This is a bit much!'

'I'm sorry if you think that I insulted you,' answered the angel, 'but I have to use a few hardy examples to get you back to basics. No, you do not have to be on your knees and no, you do not have to say your prayers. All I want from you is an open mind. Look at the sunset, how awe-inspiring this beautiful picture of mother nature is. All I want you to do is, to sit here and quietly let this beautiful view sink into your mind and soul. Use it as a tool of meditation, a tool which we will need in our dialogue. You must be prepared to develop the capacity to wonder, just like a child. It is easier to do this here than in a church or temple. The wonders of nature cannot be surpassed by the best artists in the world. Therefore I simply ask you to sit here quietly for a minute or two and take in this awe-inspiring sunset.'

'You sure have a way with words,' said Harry. 'But I agree, let's sit here for a few minutes and enjoy the sunset. You said earlier that in eternity, time is not of the essence. I can be convinced to think this way, and to prove that I can do it, I will sit here in silence for a while. However, I will look at my Rolex occasionally just to see if you're right.'

'Boy, you're a hard man to convince!' exclaimed the angel. 'You don't believe that I can make time stand still? Just be quiet for a moment and don't argue, otherwise the dried up desert cactus will never be brought to life with a little bit of the water, called "grace".'

Harry and the angel sat on the bench for a few minutes enjoying the sunset. After a few minutes Harry said, 'You are so right. This is beautiful. You know, I often drive to Whistler, but I never stop or slow down. I should really have taken more time to sit here and enjoy this miracle of nature.'

Forgetting to look at his watch to see whether time really stood still, Harry continued, 'Why don't you tell me now what you want to discuss?'

'Very well,' said the angel. 'I want to discuss twelve topics which I consider important in your life and in the life of a lot of other people. In the olden days, twelve was a magic number, a so-called code with which to explain a universal principle or multitude of people. For example, St. John in his Revelations speaks about twelve times twelve thousand people serving and worshipping the "lamb". He meant an uncountable number of people. I am not saying that what we are going to talk about covers the total mystery of God and faith in God. That would be impossible. But I chose twelve points for our discussion because I thought that it would cover a large spectrum of what is really important in the life of a person. I could have chosen many more, but I thought that the ones I selected are basic, and you don't have to be a theologian to understand them. I tried to keep complexity out of our discussions.'

Harry said, 'You sure are an eloquent angel! What are the points of our discussion?'

The angel answered, 'I want to start with my friend Pontius Pilate and answer his question and explain what truth is. Then I want to discuss love, because truth and love go hand in hand. I also want to discuss Jesus. Remember, I went through a very significant change of heart, from being one of his tormentors to one of his friends, an angel, who wants to relate that experience to others. Finally I would like to convince you, you whom I compared to "a spiritually dried up desert cactus", my apologies, please – that you have the potential to become a very important partner in building the kingdom of God. You see, I will use a few analogies that you are familiar with from your business world. And finally I want to convince you that it is wise to do God's will.'

'You make this sound quite interesting,' said Harry. 'You have convinced me to participate. You have fixed my tire. I guess I have to agree to participate in this dialogue of yours. I will try not to be too obnoxious.'

Looking at his watch which always was his normal routine when he made major decisions, Harry said, full of determination, 'Let's get to work!'

Both shook hands to seal the agreement and the angel, after a moment of silence, started with the first point of the discussion.

The Spirit of Truth

'Harry,' the angel said, 'we have to go back to the question Pontius Pilate asked Jesus. Remember during the trial Jesus indicated that he had come into the world to give witness to the truth and Pontius Pilate answered more or less cynically, "What is truth." Do you know what truth is, Harry?'

Harry thought for a moment and was confused. He told himself, *If I answer money, the angel will say money has really no value in itself. If I answer time, he will say time in eternity is of no importance. If I say the law, he will say that the law only reflects the guidelines of a system under which a community of people want to live. If I say this bench on which we sit, he will say the bench is really not made of solid stone, but of neutrinos, which cannot be seen with a naked eye or even under a microscope. They represent the borderline between energy, which has no mass, and mass itself, but they are considered the building blocks of the universe. He will argue with me about what is true until I am blue in my face. Maybe I should test the angel and tell him that I really do not know what truth is...*

Harry therefore said loudly to the angel, 'My friend, I really don't know what truth is. Truth is in the eye of the beholder; in other words, what you understand to be truth is different from what I understand. Truth is a matter of vision.'

'Right you are!' said the angel. 'The spirit of truth does not come easy; it must be nurtured in your attitude toward things and developed over many years in your mind. Still, it is the basis of any relationship you want to develop or maintain. You find the truth in yourself with proper vision. Like with a telescope, you must focus your mind on the truth. Remember the communist system in Russia?'

'Yes,' answered Harry.

'Remember the name of the communist party newspaper?'

'Yes I do. I believe the name was *Pravda*.'

'Do you know what *Pravda* means?' asked the angel.

'No, but tell me.'

'The name means "truth". The communist system was developed on a lie, the negation of the existence of God. The government named its main propaganda instrument, which was the newspaper *Pravda*, "Truth". You see, truth is very hard to define, especially when you want to use truth to foster human ideas, political movements, philosophies and thoughts. Governments justify their actions because they believe they act in the name of truth.'

'There is only one real truth,' the angel continued. 'That is a truth which every human has to face eventually. That truth is God. Whether in this life or the next, God will be the focal point for every human being.'

'But nobody has ever seen God,' said Harry angrily. 'Nobody can prove that God really exists. You know that I myself wrestled with this problem a long time. Yes, I was educated as a Catholic. I even went to a Jesuit university, but now after many years I conclude that there is no God, that in fact God is dead. He has no meaning in my life. If God is the one promoted by the religious institutions, then I had better live true to my principles and remain an atheist or at best an agnostic.'

'You remind me of a person I met once who said to me, "Thank God I am an atheist!"' the angel answered. 'Not only is such a statement absurd, but it really is critical of the messengers, the organized religious institutions which struggle to explain who God is but cannot define him. Yes, God is a mystery. God is hidden. But God can be found through the attitude of a child, not with intellect or reason. God is unthinkable. St. Augustine thought precisely about this problem when he walked on a beach in Africa. There he saw a small child. This child was making a small hole into the sand and was trying to fill it with water by using a spoon.

'St. Augustine asked this child what he was doing. And the child answered, "I am pouring the whole ocean into this little hole." "But that is impossible," said St. Augustine. "You must be out of your mind." The child answered, "It is easier to pour all the oceans of the world into this hole then it is to comprehend God." God is beyond human thought. We only get a glimpse of him through the one who came from God, Jesus the Christ.'

'You use powerful words,' countered Harry. 'You can tell me all these things; I may believe them or not. But you still cannot prove that God exists. Why, for example, are there so many different religions in this world? If God existed, he would not allow this mess we have here on earth. Most wars, for example, have been fought for religious reasons. Why would God, who is supposed to care for humanity, allow this to happen?'

'Good point, standard stuff brought forward by the average atheist,' replied the angel. 'It isn't God who instigates these wars. People start wars on the basis of what they think God should be. They want to superimpose their vision of God on others. But they don't know who God is in reality.

'Look, for example,' the angel continued, 'at these religions: Jews fight the Arabs, Christians fought Jews and Arabs, Hindus fight Muslims. All pray to the same God, in different ways. Each of these religions think that they have found their God. In reality it is actually their vision of who they think God *should* be, but not who God really *is*.'

'Well, then who is God?' asked Harry impatiently.

'*God is truth and love,*' said the angel. 'As I said before, truth and love go hand in hand. When God appeared to Moses in a bush and Moses asked who he should say sent him, a voice, the voice of God, said, "Tell them that Yahweh sent you." *Yahweh* means "I am" or "I am with you all the time". To be with you means that God is always there to care for you. You only have to realize this.'

'This is interesting,' Harry said. 'Tell me more.'

The angel answered, 'Jesus, who came from God, gave us a glimpse of who God is in reality. He is the one who can testify with authority. The Jewish people found this preposterous and blasphemous. The Romans were spiritually not trained enough to understand what Jesus stood for. They thought Jesus to be a revolutionary. Therefore when Jesus spoke of the truth, Pontius Pilate did not comprehend and simply put truth aside. He had no understanding of the truth.'

'I can see that,' said Harry. 'But how about our new scientific discoveries? So far none of the scientists have found God in their latest research.'

The angel answered, 'Scientists such as Isaac Newton,

Einstein and so many others discovered the basic laws by which the universe exists. Yes, they have not found God in their discoveries. In fact, for a long time the Roman Catholic Church was very reluctant to endorse scientific development because of fear and very narrow thinking. These scientific discoveries were hidden for a long period of time until the telescope was developed. With this instrument Galileo proved a new world system which Copernicus had developed. Until that time people believed that the earth was the center of the solar system. It created a revolution of thought when it was discovered that this was not the case. You probably know that Galileo was called before the Inquisition to revoke his findings. People were simply not prepared for what is true. They had a very narrow vision. Because of this and many other factors, people, especially the so-called intelligentsia, developed atheism as a theory. They could not combine faith with reason. Descartes, the great French philosopher said, "I think, therefore I am." He should have said, "I think *because* I am." We are not alive because we are thinking beings. We are able to think because we are alive.

'But enough of all these difficult thought processes!' the angel continued. 'I want to make you aware of another aspect of the truth.'

'And what is that?' asked Harry. 'I thought there was only one truth!'

'Yes, you are right,' answered the angel. 'But this is also a very important aspect of God's truth, namely that the truth lives in you as a spark of God's spirit. You are made in God's image and a spark of God's spirit lives in your soul, not only in yours but in every other person's soul. This spark is like a grain; it can wither away and bring no fruit; it also can be fertilized with God's grace, for example, to bring ample fruit. Whether or not the grain comes to full fruition, it still is embedded in every human soul.'

'This is hard to comprehend,' said Harry. 'You mean that I have a spark of God's spirit imprinted on my soul? This is something I was not aware of, and if you ask a lot of other people, they won't be able to comprehend this either.'

'Yes,' said the angel, 'God's spirit lives in you and in every other human being. You, as well as everyone else, have an eternal soul, a soul destined to eternal life. Everyone has the capacity to love. *God is love.* By definition, therefore, if you love God or your neighbor, you bring God's spirit alive in yourself. That is a very important principle of any relationship, whether with God or with other human beings.'

'You sure sound very convincing!' said Harry. 'Tell me more… I never thought about God in the way you explained it. You mean the love I had for Beatrice years ago was a spark of God's spirit?'

'Say it as you wish,' answered the angel. 'Love comes with many faces. I think we have to talk about love. We must understand what love is. Love is so hard to comprehend because we are influenced by so many other impressions surrounding us. But in order to understand God, we must define love. Without understanding love based on truth, we will not be able to comprehend God, if that is possible.

'Let's go back to your relationship with Beatrice and see whether you, in your own words, can define love.'

The Spirit of Love

'Harry,' the angel asked, 'were you ever in love with Beatrice? I know this is a personal question, and it may not be fair to ask this question. You don't have to answer if you don't want to.'

Harry recalled how he had met Beatrice. It was on a rainy evening in Montreal in the early fall. The leaves were turning into the fall colors of yellow and red. It was relatively mild but crisp. He had just arrived at the Montreal airport from a trip to the USA where he had visited an uncle. He had been waiting for a taxi, and so had Beatrice. Since he had been short of money, he had simply asked her whether she would like to share the cost of a taxi ride. He had been very flustered and apologetic about his request and for a short time his whole self-confidence was shot to pieces. This had never happened to him before. His self-assurance gone, he had wanted to open the taxi door, but could not because of his nervousness. The rain had been plastering down on his head and Beatrice had held her umbrella over his head to keep him dry. Still, rain water had run down his neck, making him uncomfortably wet. He had felt like a wet poodle and said so. Beatrice had laughed at this comparison and said that this look suited him quite well.

They had started a conversation and were still talking when the taxi delivered Harry to his destination. He had paid his share of the fare and left without asking for her name or asking whether they could meet again. At home that evening, he had thought a long time about this young lady whom he had just met and who had touched his heart. The more he thought the more he had the desire to meet her again. He had been so impressed by her simple elegance, the ease with which he could communicate with her, her innocence and openness.

She is a natural beauty, he thought. *I must meet her again. But how?* He had looked out of the window into the rainy night and carried on, *If she is interested in a relationship, then she might respond to a small ad which I will put in the local newspaper...* The next morning he had published an ad which read:

> Wet poodle, fully dry now, wants to continue the conversation with the lovely lady who came to the rescue last night at the airport.

He had thought that there could only be one person who would understand this ad. He had never really expected a reply. But Beatrice had answered the ad. And so a relationship had developed, culminating in marriage.

'Yes,' was Harry's answer to the angel's question. 'Yes, I was in love with Beatrice.'

'What was your first impression of this feeling of love?' asked the angel.

'My first impression was,' answered Harry, 'that love is beautiful, that it is an indescribable feeling of elation, energy and joy. Suddenly you find somebody with whom you can share your innermost thoughts.'

'That is nicely said,' said the angel, 'but continue.'

'I was in love,' Harry continued, 'because I found in Beatrice a person with whom I could talk intelligently and share my true feelings. She was beautiful, and I believe she still is. I was attracted to her sexually and spiritually. She made me feel like a real man. You must realize I came from a family where the word love was never spoken. My parents were busy making a living scraping by. It was hard in those days. They had a small business and their only desire was to make money and have a secure retirement. They never showed any affection to each other and lived side by side as strangers. Here, in Beatrice, I found a woman with whom I could bare my soul. I could talk about things I never could talk about with my parents or friends. Beatrice gave me more security than she ever thought.'

After a brief silence Harry said, 'I pretended to be self-assured but was not really. I pretended to know everything but I really didn't. My insecurity culminated in the pretense of being "macho", showing off things which really do not matter. Beatrice saw through this farce. We sometimes had terrible arguments about what was important and what was not. I never would concede that I had lost an argument. I thought it was not "man-like" to give in.'

'Why do I tell you all these things?' Harry continued. 'Is it so important to bare my soul in front of you, you who are a stranger to me?'

'Yes it is,' answered the angel. 'Please carry on.'

Harry said, 'Right now I am so confused that I ask myself the question why I ever married Beatrice. I don't know whether Beatrice ever loved me!'

'Never mind,' said the angel, 'you don't have to get sentimental. I am here for a reason. The reason is to make your marriage blossom again and help you find, through faith and trust in God's love, what is really important in both of your lives.

'Harry,' the angel continued, 'your first impression when you fell in love with Beatrice was that love must be beautiful. You felt passion and desire for Beatrice; you felt joy when you saw her; you felt that you could not live without her.'

Harry answered, 'You said it, and I am sad to say that this feeling is gone.'

'How did you express your love?' asked the angel.

Harry said, 'Naturally we made passionate love, culminating in a wonderful, indescribable feeling of togetherness and unity. However the desire died after a few years because we became complacent. The act of lovemaking became routine. The spark of passion was gone.'

'It's interesting,' the angel said, 'that you describe your passion for Beatrice as unifying. In fact God wants you to be one in spirit and flesh. Did you know that this is God's will?'

'I never thought about it,' answered Harry. 'It never occurred to me that God was interested in sex. At least that was the message I received when I went to church. Sex was never discussed; it was taboo. It was at best classified as a procreating act, and compared more with unnecessary lust than with the total self-giving and unity I experienced when we both made love.'

The angel said, 'What you say about passion and unity is wonderful. I see signs of life in you. Did you know that the greatest commandment Jesus gave us is to love?'

'Yes,' said Harry, 'but I always thought that God's love was based on charity and sacrifice – never sex or passion!'

'You have the wrong impression of the love God wants!' said the angel. 'God wants you to express the love he commands you to have as the love for your neighbor first and foremost. Your closest neighbor is your spouse. This is a sign of unity and this unity can truly be pleasurable.'

The angel continued, 'But you can express your love to Beatrice also in other ways, not only in passion. You can express your love by sharing your thoughts, trust, friendliness, openness, and acceptance. You can express your love daily by simply being your true self and helping Beatrice to be the best spouse you could ever have. Love is expressed in the little things in the daily life, not in great material gifts. The latter may be sometimes just an excuse or cover-up for failure.

'As a true lover you want to make your marriage as successful as possible,' the angel continued. 'That is hard work and commands commitment and humility by yourself and your spouse.'

'You speak like wise old man,' Harry said. 'It really isn't easy to have a happy marriage, especially when you discover after many years that your interests diverge. You said it rightly; it is hard work to be happy!'

The angel said, 'Harry, you were quite open with me in your thoughts. We must carry on in our discussion about God and Jesus. I used the example of your marriage to find out what you think love is all about. You sure have the capacity to love and to understand what God wants from you. We said earlier on that to find God is to love. Let's discuss in more detail the love of God manifested and made flesh in Jesus.'

God, Love Infinite

'Thank you for describing so well the love you had once for Beatrice,' the angel carried on. 'You were very open with me. This was great. Your first impression was that this love was beautiful and fulfilling. It was based on trust and openness. You used the word unity quite often. Do you think that God's love can be compared to this love, or do you feel that God's love is much different?'

Harry said, 'I never thought of God in terms of love. In my early youth I thought of God as the creating power far removed from humanity. But now as a confessed atheist or agnostic I cannot concede that God exists. If I believe that God exists, then I cannot bring love and creative power into a cohesive balance. One must supersede the other.

'You see,' Harry continued, 'when you are a lover, you commit yourself unconditionally to someone else, and by committing yourself you become vulnerable. How can you combine the idea that God is the creative power, a power which is unthinkable, with the vulnerability of a lover?'

'That is a good point,' the angel answered. 'Yes, God is the creative power of all that exists but surpassing this creative power is his love. His love is stronger and more powerful than all the creation you can see or even imagine.'

'These are mighty words you use,' said Harry, rather subdued. 'You say that God's love surpasses even the marvels of the universe?'

'Yes,' said the angel, 'otherwise his only begotten son, Jesus the Christ, would not have sacrificed his life freely for the redemption of the whole of humanity. When God created humanity, he gave man the power to think freely and the ability to accept or not to accept God. He gave humanity the ability to make a choice to love or not to love. He always thought that love was stronger than anything else. The sacrifice of Jesus on the cross is the proof that love is stronger than anything else.

'You see,' continued the angel, 'before the universe was created, God's love existed. The universe is limited by time; God's love is eternal, without borders or restriction of time. Therefore God's love is greater than what you see or not see, what you can imagine or not imagine.'

'This is quite interesting,' remarked Harry, again rather subdued. 'I really was not aware of the immensity of God's love, especially his love for the whole humanity. I always thought that the God whom I had faith in during my youth had forgotten humanity. This is one of the many reasons why I turned into an atheist or an agnostic.'

He continued, 'I couldn't understand how, if God exists, and he had any power at all or had any interest in the fate of humanity, why he would allow these wars, and all the poverty and inequality in the world to happen. That is why I completely shut God out of my life and turned my attention to creating wealth for myself. At least I can touch it. God's love, as you describe it, I cannot touch!'

The angel said: 'I knew there was hope for you. You have the capacity to love, the real "ultimate" in this life. The things you learned in your youth and even the happy memories of your early marriage are still on your mind. This is good news!

'But let's carry on with the faith that God's love is without borders,' the angel continued. 'The Jews in the Old Testament had a close relationship with God, a relationship based on the law given by Moses. They sometimes saw God as a burden because he put them through trials, tribulations and exiles. Also their relationship was more distant. They would not pronounce or spell the word *God*. When Jesus taught that we could call God *'Our Father'*, they thought that this was blasphemy. Jesus was really the one who brought humanity and the faithful into a totally new, much fuller relationship with the all-powerful God. And that relationship is based on love.'

Harry asked, 'How did Jesus do this? Was this through the cross or through his teaching?'

'Both,' answered the angel. 'Jesus did this through the cross as the ultimate sacrifice and through his teaching to make people aware that there is a loving, caring God to whom we can relate anytime through prayer.'

His interest awakened, Harry asked, 'How did Jesus tell his followers about the infinite love of God?'

'Mainly through his parables, but also through his example,' the angel replied. 'There are many parables which show the love of God. For example, the parable of the prodigal son. It should really be called the parable of the prodigal father, a father who is almost too wasteful with his love. The father is the one who greets the son he thought was lost unconditionally and spontaneously. The joy that the son, who squandered everything, came back, is so immense that the father immediately celebrates with his whole household. This is the gospel's gospel. Joy becomes overflowing when those who are lost come back. That is an example of boundless, unconditional love.'

The angel continued, 'There are other parables which show the unending love and patience of God the Father. Remember the parable of the fig tree. The owner of the tree wants to cut it down because it does not bring fruit. The gardener, who represents God, says to the owner, "Let's wait a little while and fertilize the tree, with grace that is, and the tree will come back to life, bring fruit and so will be saved." You see once you understand more clearly the love of God, you will want to come back because you will be filled with his energy and love in yourself. Every day will be joyful.'

Harry was a now speechless – unusual for a brash self-assured businessman who usually had answers for everything. His whole mind was in upheaval. He had never thought of God's love as the angel expressed it so clearly. To him love was still more a sign of being vulnerable than an absolute necessity to develop a relationship either with God or with his wife Beatrice. He was too self-centered to understand real love and it was not easy to overcome his doubts. But his defenses were weakened.

Harry said, 'You sure can explain the parables to me in a way that they make sense even to a professed atheist. Is there any hope for me?'

The angel answered, 'Of course, and not only for you, but for everyone else. Look at me; I was one of the people who crucified

Christ and I am not in hell. In fact I am alive and well and live in the full vision of God, which is heaven.

'But let me show you a few more examples of how God's love works. There is the parable about the vineyard owner who hires people to help him in the vineyard. The people who were hired last, just shortly before sundown, received the same reward as the people who worked the whole day. I guess the current union mentality would not allow this and it would be called unjust. But this is God's justice which is based on love unending. There are so many other parables which reveal the love of God for the whole humanity. I only want to describe a few because we want to cover other subjects too.'

The angel continued, 'To sum it up, Jesus came as the healer of the broken-hearted and to forgive sins, not as the one who condemned humanity. Jesus the Christ, the one sent by God to earth, came to reveal that God's love is unending, patient, not based on man's justice and it is unconditional. You yourself said that this kind of love can be beautiful.'

'Then why did Jesus have to die on the cross, when God's love is so well explained in the parables and so easy and comforting for the listeners to understand?' asked Harry. 'I don't see the necessity of the sacrifice as proof that God loves humanity.'

'Well,' said the angel, 'Jesus wanted to prove that he was capable of fulfilling the Father's wish and show the ultimate act of love, which is to die for all whom he loved. Jesus said clearly, "There is no greater act of love than to give up your life for those whom you love." Jesus loved all humans, the sinners and the righteous, the believers and the non-believers, simply everyone.'

The angel continued, 'This sacrifice is the seal of approval of the new covenant between God and mankind, the reconciliation between God and humanity, the redemption of all men and women. In order to prove this statement we must continue our dialogue and discuss the person Jesus the Christ in more detail, who he was and is. Remember though, what we discuss is all a matter of faith; it is not a matter of reason. If you do not have the capacity to listen with the mind of a child who simply stands there in wonder and awe, you will not comprehend the fullness of this truth.'

Jesus, Son of God, Son of Man

Harry sat on the bench in silence for a while trying to understand what the angel had just explained. For him, a man who had lived a self-centered life, God's love the way it had been explained was incomprehensible. He had never loved selflessly, but only on the basis of 'What is in it for me?' Yes, in the first years of their marriage, he had been in love with Beatrice because he had found her very sensuous and attractive. For him, a little overweight and balding, to have such a beautiful wife was a status symbol. He had achieved early in life the dreams he had in his youth, money, an attractive, intelligent and sensuous wife and a family to be admired by neighbors. But unconditional love, as the angel had described God's love, did not exist for him. He looked at marriage as a profitable partnership, profitable for him.

While Harry sat in thoughtful silence, the angel started to talk again. 'Harry,' the angel said, 'we must now discuss the person of Jesus the Christ in more detail. Who do you think Jesus was in reality?'

'Well,' said Harry, 'I know that Jesus is a historical figure. I believe he was mentioned two or three times by various Jewish and Roman historians. Since they mentioned him and are reliable sources, I must assume he really did live and is not a figment of our imagination. Also his birth is the date from which we measure time.'

The angel said, 'Yes, you are right. Jesus is mentioned by various historians. But we do not want to look at the historical Jesus. We want to look at Jesus the Christ as the center of faith. If we want to find out who Jesus the Christ really is, then we must put human reasoning away and look at him through the eyes of a believer. We must look at him for what he stood for and what he died for. We must look at him with a mindset of awe for God's plan of salvation.

'These words may be overwhelming,' the angel continued. 'I

hope that this discussion will not be too difficult for you to understand, because I still see in you the doubting Thomas, a person who is not easily convinced and who is too stubborn to move from his entrenched position.'

'Why don't you try me?' said Harry. 'I have already turned into an agnostic after the first few discussions which we had. I see already some new possibilities, and maybe "Harry the blind" will eventually get his eyes opened!'

'I hope I can do this,' said the angel bursting out in laughter. 'I see you have a sense of humor, always a good sign of openness and willingness.'

The angel continued, 'The real nature of Jesus the Christ cannot be explained with reason. God is beyond human thinking and reasoning. Therefore we must approach Jesus the Christ with faith. In the gospels, Jesus never says that he is God; others, either the apostles or first believers called him the *Son of God*. Many times saintly or holy people were called *Sons of God*. Therefore this expression is not unique to Jesus. However, it is unique that Jesus testified that he is *One* with *God* his father, that he is filled with God's spirit to the fullest and that he is the only one to fully know God. He is the truth and testifies to the truth. He spoke these powerful words with authority. Many people believed him.'

After a brief moment the angel said, 'One of the fundamentals of the Christian faith is the faith in the Trinity, God the creator, God the begotten son, and God the spirit proceeding from both. To describe the mystery of the Trinity is impossible, but in human terminology the Trinity could be compared to life, love and light. These are wonderful descriptions.'

Harry said, 'I guess this was very difficult for people to believe, that a man, a carpenter's son, a neighbor and family member, declared and taught that he was the second person of the Holy Trinity.'

The angel said, 'The faith in the mystery of the Holy Trinity was only developed over a period of time, many years after the death of Jesus. It is too difficult to understand, and beyond comprehension for the human mind. Therefore we must leave it as such and continue our journey to understand the other nature of Jesus the Christ which is related to his humanity. It is a matter of faith that Jesus the Christ has a divine and human nature.'

'I guess it is much easier to relate to a real human being than to the mystery of how you describe the Trinity,' said Harry. 'How do you see Jesus's human nature?'

The angel said, 'Jesus is the focal point of all humanity, whether for believers or for non-believers, whether for saints or sinners, whether in this life or the next. Jesus is the one who embraces all humanity in his nature. The expression *Son of Man* is an old biblical description of the one who will come to be the Messiah and the redeemer of humanity. Jesus uses this description for himself a few times in the gospel. His sacrifice on the cross includes all humanity – past, present and future.'

The angel continued, 'Every human being has an eternal soul. The soul is God's creation. Therefore to be a human, male or female, is expressed foremost in the human soul, which is eternal and which is a spark of God's life, love and light in all.'

Harry said, 'You make it easy to understand. If it is so easy, then why is it that so many theologians doubt the nature of Jesus, doubt his mission, and see in him a spirit or a fiction or a religious fanatic? Look at the latest Jesus movement, a movement which analyses biblical texts. I understand this movement is sponsored by theologians, university teachers and other religious leaders. They say that it is doubtful that a lot of what was written in the bible about Jesus was really spoken by him. They say that the only two authentic words spoken by him were "Our Father". The rest were insinuations or reflections.'

'You are right,' answered the angel. 'The bible has been demystified by many scholars and theologians. They are searching for the historical Jesus. You cannot dissect Jesus's teaching like you dissect a dead carcass. Jesus, the Son of Man is embedded in the history of salvation as foretold in the Old Testament. We must see in Jesus the Messiah, the reason why the scriptures were written in the first place. He is the one who fulfilled the prophecies of the Old Testament and the law of Moses.'

'Then why did the Jews not believe and why do they not believe now?' asked Harry. 'If you say that the Jews were the first people to receive the message of redemption of humanity, then why do they not believe?'

The angel said, 'I cannot speak for the Jewish people. I do not know the reasons. Maybe they cannot imagine that the Messiah has two natures, one divine and one human; maybe they think that the Messiah, as promised long ago, is only destined for the Jewish people, not for the world at large. God is a matter of vision and faith. You will receive a complete vision of God after your death and then you will fully understand.'

Harry said, 'I don't understand everything you have said. I never thought much about religion, especially not about theology. May I ask you a question?'

'By all means!' said the angel. 'What would you like to know?'

'Why was it necessary that Jesus had to redeem the world through his sacrifice on the cross?'

The angel answered, 'Let me explain this to you right now.'

Jesus, the Victor over Evil

The angel asked Harry, 'Do you believe that Satan exists?'

Harry answered, 'This is a funny question. Remember I am a so-called atheist or agnostic. I have my doubts about whether God really exists. And here you are asking me whether I believe that Satan exists or whether he is fiction? I can visualize that he exists because I see so many things wrong in this world. I guess there must be somebody who is a spoiler, somebody who disrupts, somebody who influences humanity to destroy, kill and hate. If God is a mystery, then so is evil.'

'Yes, evil is also a mystery,' said the angel. 'Evil goes back to before the universe was created. Evil is based on defiance of the goodness of God. Evil is based on a lie. The Prince of Darkness, Satan or the devil, whatever name you want to use, has the ability to make a lie or untruth believable. Every aspect of evil is directed against God, and by implication against the dignity of a human person.' He paused. 'Should I explain this in more detail?'

'Yes, that would be great!' answered Harry. 'I really have no conception of what you are talking about. To me this sounds very abstract. My understanding of evil was always that to have fun in life is evil; pleasure is evil, maybe even greed is evil, even though I firmly believe that greed is good. I will be very interested in what you have to say about what evil is.'

The angel said, 'Let me go back in time, in fact to before time existed, before the universe was even created. Lucifer was one of the great angels serving God. He had a perfect vision of God. He, unlike all humanity, could fully comprehend God's power, light and love. He especially resented love because true love, which is by definition unconditionally caring and sharing in community and unity, can make you vulnerable. As a true lover, you are giving something freely and unconditionally to somebody else. This also implies that you are vulnerable because the risk is that the one whom you love may not accept your love.

'Lucifer was not prepared to respond unconditionally to God's love. He was too self-centered and proud. He rebelled and was cast out of heaven, which means from the light of God's vision into the eternal darkness. Lucifer, which really means the carrier of light, was evicted from heaven because of his pride and will remain forever in darkness.'

Harry asked, 'How does Jesus relate to the events you just described?'

The angel answered, 'Lucifer, or the devil, still roams around like a prowling lion. As the Prince of Darkness and as the father of lies or untruths, he has the ability to present to humanity what is evil and bad as good, what are lies as truth, what is hate and greed as good and so on. Jesus the Christ was sent into this world to bear witness to what is really true, what is really good and what is really love. As the utmost testimony to God's truth, he gave his life on the cross, the ultimate sacrifice anybody can do if he or she is truly in love.

'You see,' continued the angel, 'Jesus the Christ had complete faith in his mission, faith in the Father's will, the ultimate faith any human can have. Jesus the Christ died on the cross as a human being as a sacrifice for all humanity. He demonstrated the ability that even humans can carry out the commandment of ultimate and unconditional love. The full realization of his divinity, his equality with God and his nature of the begotten son of God, came at the point of his death and his resurrection from the dead. Through his sacrifice on the cross as a human, a death freely chosen as the culmination of his mission on earth, he destroyed evil and the result of evil, which is death.'

Harry said, 'It must have been hard for the devil to realize that a human, a being which is by definition inferior to him, was victorious over him. That must have hurt his pride.'

The angel said, 'Yes, but be wary of the devil especially because of his ability to make you believe that a lie is to be the truth. The devil, because of Jesus's ultimate sacrifice on the cross which resulted in his defeat, hates humanity. The devil wants to destroy humanity at all costs.'

'You mean that this is the reason why we have so many wars, famines, earthquakes and the likes?' asked Harry.

'I doubt that earthquakes, famines and floods are the devil's work. Remember that the devil is a spirit just like God or the angels. The devil pollutes the minds of people – generations of people, or even whole countries – with untruths and lies. That process may take years or centuries. Remember time is of no essence in eternity.'

Harry asked, 'Do you have some examples that demonstrate your theory? I would be very interested to know more about how evil exists in this world.'

'That is not to difficult to demonstrate,' said the angel. 'Since the devil hates humanity, every one of his acts is directed towards destroying humans. Let's look at a few cases which demonstrate the ability to make truth to be untruth or in other words to make a lie believed to be true.'

'Remember slavery? In the olden days, slavery was part of a culture or even a necessity for the ruling class to maintain a certain living standard. Slavery was accepted and even promoted everywhere in the world. Slaves were considered a subclass of people who had no rights or dignity. They could be discarded or sold like a chattel. If you believe that each human being is equal before God because of his or her eternal soul, which is a spark of God's living spirit, then slavery must be evil.

'Even the Christian institutions are not free from evil acts. For example, the Inquisition instituted by the Roman Catholic Church for centuries was an attack against human freedom and human dignity. The Church tried to play God and judge like God. She justified political, earthly goals with what was assumed to be God's will. How can you argue with one who pretends to speak in the name of God? The only argument you have is to look at the result, the fruits of such a policy. The result was enormous suffering by people who did not agree with the teaching of the Church but did live according to what they thought was right. The act of condemning them was evil. It was an act against their dignity as humans. Human justice was applied, not God's justice.

'But let's look at more recent events, which definitely demonstrate the power of evil in this world. It is, of course, the Holocaust, an event where evil showed its ultimate power. The Holocaust was a result of ideas and actions developed over a long period of time. It was the culmination of evil which had evolved from generations of Christian culture. When reading the descriptions of the event of the crucifixion, the reader can be influenced to think that the Jews were responsible for the death of Jesus the Christ. It was God's plan since the beginning of time to redeem humanity and destroy evil through this act of ultimate love. If at all, then the whole humanity bears the fault, not only the Jews. This wrong mindset created over the years a relationship of non-acceptance by the Gentiles. The Jews were always outcasts, especially in Christian Europe.

'Nazism was influenced by the philosophies of the nineteenth century, especially those which propagated the pre-eminence of the state over the individual person. During the same time Nietzsche, a German atheist and philosopher, thought that eventually a super-race would develop, eliminating the need for faith in a God who did not exist anyway.

'All these theories are lies,' the angel continued. 'But they were used as an argument to destroy the Jews in Europe. Through complete control of the media and the information channels, ordinary people were bombarded with this untruth, day in, day out. Jews were classified as subhuman, not equal to the German master race. They could be destroyed in the most efficient way without recourse to a consciously made moral or ethical evaluation. It was an evil act, an act based on a lie deemed to be good, but utterly bad.

'Do you want to know more about other evil acts which are propagated as good for humanity and which are carried out as a so-called service to humanity, but which are based on a lie?' asked the angel.

'Just one more!' said Harry. 'I think I get the picture. I am quite interested in what you classify as evil in our day and time.'

The angel answered, 'The greatest evil we face right now is abortion. The abortionists propagate abortion as a service to humanity. They kill and destroy the most defenseless and innocent human being, a flower of humanity which will never have a chance to bloom. Their act is based on an untruth, on a lie. Abortion is not only against the will and law of God but also against the dignity of humans who could have blossomed but cannot. God is the greatest propagator of human dignity. All his laws are given to protect the human race and dignity. The untruth propagated by the abortionists is that an act against the dignity of the human race is deemed to be a service to humans. The evil act of killing is advertised as a good thing. A lie is made to be perceived to be true.'

'I never thought about it in this way!' said Harry. 'I myself contemplated abortion, but my wife Beatrice was against it. Come to think of it, that was the start of our marriage falling apart. Interesting!'

The angel continued, 'Harry, you are an economist; you are a businessmen who sees value. What would you say if your most valuable resource, with which your living standard is maintained and which will provide you with a future pension when you are old, is destroyed? Would you say that this is an act to be encouraged or discouraged?'

Harry said, 'I sure would not encourage such an act because I like my comfort and I sure like to have security in my old age.'

'Well,' said the angel, 'abortion is the destruction of human beings; abortion also kills those who might have provided you with a living standard you would want to have in your old age. If you kill the future of a country through abortion, then one way or another an economic price will have to be paid. You see, abortion is like a holocaust of humanity, the killing of humans not protected by the law of the land. Abortion also has an economic impact on the future of the country, never mind the moral issues.'

Harry said, 'I think we have talked enough about evil. Let's carry on!'

'As you wish,' said the angel. 'Yes, there is evil in this world – evil which humans may not be aware of because they do not have the full vision of God's presence in their lives and do not understand God's will. Jesus the Christ is the victor over evil through his death on the cross. He also is the redeemer of the world through his great love for humanity expressed in his desire to forgive sins. Let us talk about this now.'

Jesus, the Forgiver of Sins

The angel asked, 'Harry, do you know what sin is?'

Harry said, 'This has always been a subject which I have misunderstood. I really don't know what a sin is and I am sure that a lot of people do not understand sin either. The only thing I correlate to sin is guilt and I hate guilt! So tell me what a sin is.'

The angel said, 'God gave ten commandments to Moses. These commandments are like a path on which to travel safely. But what do these commandments achieve or supposed to achieve, Harry?'

Harry answered, 'I suppose if you follow the commandments, you please God and do the will of God. What bothers me, though, is that most of the commandments start with a negative, that is "you shall not". It is a rather stern lecture, and I can visualize a very authoritarian Father waving a finger and saying, "If you do this sin, I will remember it and will punish you for what you have done. This will teach you a lesson not to do it again."'

The angel said, 'Poor Harry, this is a complete misunderstanding of the Ten Commandments and what God wants from you. First of all, let me assure you that God is *not* an accountant who judges you on the basis of how many times you sinned. Second, God is not revengeful. If you think that way, you still have not understood that *God is Love*. If you are a lover, you don't count the failings of the one you love. If that were the case, you would not be a lover; you would be a stern judge who would calculate all the penalties and make you suffer under these penalties as just reward.'

Harry said, 'You say God is not just?'

'Of course God is just!' answered the angel. 'But his justice is based on mercy and love. You see if you had a full vision of God and fully understood the love God has for you, you would simply fulfill freely the commandments which God has given. But since your mind is touched and influenced by all the events surrounding you and your thinking is influenced by the way you were brought up, sins or failings are part of daily life.'

'Then what is a sin?' asked Harry.

The angel answered, 'You commit a sin if you fail to love, and love means to help develop the best in your neighbor whoever that should be. Your neighbor could be your wife, your father, mother, your son, your daughter, a stranger... anybody you meet. If you love your neighbor fully, you would simply do what is best for him or her. But this love is incomplete in this world because of your lack of understanding God. Therefore sin does exist. Sin is failing to carry out the commandment to love your neighbor and to love God.'

Harry said, 'How can I love God if I do not believe that God exists, or as an agnostic be uncommitted to the existence or non-existence of God?'

The angel answered, 'You can express your love to God in your love to your neighbor. Jesus classifies as hypocrites those who say, "Dear God, I love you very much. I praise and thank you, day in, day out, even on my knees in church, for the great insight I have in loving you,' but then commit acts against their neighbors which are not based on love but based on greed, self-regard, egotism or whatever. To love is hard work; but it is pleasant and pleasurable. Love is the source of happiness, but it demands discipline and commitment.'

Harry said, 'That is a very generic statement. You say that if I do not love my wife Beatrice, then I am sinning?'

'Yes, that is right!' said the angel. 'We said before, that your closest neighbor is your wife. In fact she is more than a neighbor ever will be; she is your best friend, your lover, the one who cares for you. It is God's commandment to love her to the best of your ability.'

'What happens if she does not love me?' asked Harry. 'What happens if we both decide to have a divorce. Is that also a sin?'

'It could be,' answered the angel, 'because you also have a responsibility to your children, who are dependent on you.'

Harry said, 'I don't want to go further into these discussions. These are my personal problems, and one way or another I will settle them. I wish to carry on in the discussion. You said that

Jesus will forgive our sins, that we should have faith in his generosity and simply carry on in our way of life?'

'Don't be too fast in this statement!' said the angel. 'Yes, you should have faith in the redeeming power of Jesus, but you also have to repent and have the intention of correcting your way of life.

'You see,' the angel carried on, 'God's love is so strong that he wants all human beings to share in his light and vision. As atonement for the sins of all humanity, Jesus sacrificed himself freely on the cross. This act of love was so strong and victorious that it overcame death. Through this act of love, all humanity became destined to inherit heaven, which is the eternal vision of God. It is not only vision, but God's sharing of his divinity with you in community with all humanity. I know this is hard to understand. We will discuss this subject a little bit later. In the meantime I would like you to be assured of the redeeming power of Jesus's death on the cross. Christ died for all humanity, past, present and future. Therefore as a beginning of your journey back to understanding the love of God, you must have faith that Jesus will forgive your trespasses or sins, either in this life or the next.'

Harry said, 'Well spoken! Whenever I think about the forgiveness of sins, I think about confession. I used to go to confession when I was younger, and in all fairness I hated it. Here I was rattling down sins like from a catalogue. I was neither convinced that what I told the priest was a sin, nor did I believe that I should tell my innermost thoughts to a person for whom I had very little respect.'

The angel said, 'Your feelings or opinions towards a priest are not material in confessing your sins. To be a priest is a ministry, an office. The priest acts like an agent of God. Jesus delegated the power to forgive sins to his apostles, and they in turn delegated this authority to the ones who came after them. By the way, the Roman Catholic Church also changed the terminology of confession. It is not called anymore an "act of penance", with its negative implication; it is called an "act of reconciliation". You, by confessing the wrongs you have done against the commandment of love, will be reconciled in the spirit to God. With this reconciliation, the spark of God's spirit which lives in you will grow and blossom.'

Harry said, 'You sure have a way with words! You must have been a romantic when you lived on this earth!'

'Could be!' said the angel with a smile. 'But what I want to share with you is the evolution of my thinking from a soldier who was trained to kill, who never ever thought about the beauty of true love to a lover through the grace of God. All people have the capacity to evolve from a heartless soldier or profiteer to a lover who shares, from a taker to a giver, from a sinner who lives in darkness to a person who realizes that a spark of God's love lives in his or her soul. That is the redeeming power of Jesus. Is this not great?'

'Well,' said Harry, 'you sound convincing. You have made me think about the beginning of my marriage when I was happy. I loved Beatrice. We did not have much; what we had, we shared. We lived in the unity you so often bring up in this dialogue. Yes, those were happy times and sometimes I wish I could have them back.'

The angel exclaimed, 'Harry, I see a light at the end of the tunnel, literally speaking! There is hope for you as there is for everyone else. All you need to do is to reflect a little bit, search and acknowledge where you went wrong. It was probably not only you: it was probably the fault of both of you. The first step to a reconciliation is the acknowledgment of where you went wrong.'

'You sound like a marriage counselor!' said Harry rather jokingly. 'But let's carry on with our discussion. I am finding our talk more and more interesting. In all fairness, in the beginning I didn't really take you seriously and was afraid we would have a long, boring discussion about the existence of God and how that faith in God is transmitted through the ages by the religious institutions and churches.'

'You seem to be so very critical of religious institutions!' said the angel. 'They have had a tough time, just as much as everyone else, in presenting the reality of God in our daily life. It is one thing to teach this reality; it is another thing to live it. The last part is so difficult. But as I said before, have faith in the redeeming power of Jesus. His sacrifice is the ultimate act of forgiveness. Jesus was not a coward; he did not abandon humanity to the power of evil. He gave us the ultimate gift, his life for all humanity. It is a mystery, an act which cannot be judged with human thought and understanding; it can only be judged through the eyes of God. And that remains to be a mystery or if you want to be more prosaic, his secret.

'Harry,' the angel continued, 'we now have to discuss the fruits of the sacrifice of Jesus which was his resurrection from the dead. As I told you, I was a witness of the resurrection, an unbelieving witness; therefore I am impartial. Shall we go on to the next subject?'

'Yes!' said Harry. 'You won't believe it, but I am really looking forward to your thoughts on the resurrection. This sure is controversial. Be prepared; I am not going to be easily convinced!'

'Don't worry!' said the angel with a smile. 'You might surprise yourself. You will realize suddenly that you, whom I called a spiritually dried up desert cactus, will rejoice in the energy flowing from your faith into the risen Christ.'

Jesus, Risen from the Dead

This was proving an exhausting discussion both for the angel and Harry. Both relaxed for a moment and were lost in their own thoughts. The sun had not moved at all. It was still sitting low over the mountainous islands to the west of the lookout. Strangely enough, there was not a single sound from the highway going north to Whistler or traffic going south to Vancouver. Everything was quiet – the sound of silence, appreciated by so many people but drowned out in the noise of daily life, a sound which invites people to meditation and prayer. Lost in his thoughts, Harry closed his eyes for a moment, and a new feeling of energy and happiness came over him. He suddenly felt rejuvenated and joyful, a joy which he had never known or had long forgotten.

He thought, *The angel is right; there may be a spark of God's spirit in my soul. This might actually be the wonderful energy, which is so unused and unrecognized, which believers call the love of God. Maybe there is hope for me, even if I do resent the fact that I am called a spiritually dried up desert cactus! I will have to talk about this to the angel.*

Aloud, Harry said to angel, 'You're a nice guy and I find you very interesting and what you say makes a lot of sense, but why did you call me a spiritually dried up desert cactus? I am alive and well; I eat and drink well, and live a good life. I still resent the comment!'

The angel had expected this, and he said with a smile, 'As I told you before, you, Harry, have a role to play in building the kingdom of God just as much as everyone else on this earth. Yes, spiritually you were dried up, you had no concept of what this kingdom is all about. Our dialogue is supposed to help you to get your life back in order and help you find out what is really important. Harry, you love the "ultimate". You demonstrate that in your daily life. You drive the "ultimate driving machine"; you have the ultimate fetish which is an expensive watch for every day of the week; you have so much money that you want to find the ultimate hiding place to keep it away from the government; you made an ultimate killing in the stock market by selling short a couple of hundred thousand shares in a gold mine which was involved in a big swindle. But you have missed one ultimate which surpasses everything you own or want to own!'

'And what is that?' asked Harry.

'That is your faith in the risen Christ – Jesus the Christ, risen from the dead and lifted into heaven and therefore opening up heaven for all, even all the spiritually dried up desert cactuses of this world!

'You see,' said the angel, 'the death of Jesus on the cross is, of course, the ultimate sacrifice, but his death would have been in vain if he had not resurrected from the dead. St. Paul says in one of his letters that if Jesus had not risen from the dead and therefore destroyed death, our faith in him would have been null and void. The death of Jesus on the cross must be seen under the light of his resurrection. If Jesus had not resurrected from death, then the faith in him would have been a fraud. Therefore the reality of the faith in Jesus the Christ hinges all in all on his resurrection, the final act of victory over evil, the fruit of which is death.'

Harry said rather reluctantly, 'Well, let me tell you, there is so much controversy over the resurrection of Jesus – people just do not believe that such an act is possible. Further, they say that Jesus was not really dead, that he was taken still alive from the cross by his followers. They say that he lived for years in hiding and died as an old man. Even theologians doubt the story of the empty grave. They cannot comprehend the bodily resurrection. They say it must be seen as a spiritual event, very abstract, very unreal. What do you say to that, my friend?'

The angel answered, 'Just like many other miracles or acts of God, this is something beyond human understanding and is a matter of faith.' He continued, 'You again have to look at the resurrection under the light of the history of salvation which started already with the creation of the universe but became apparent with the creation of human beings. All human beings have an eternal soul which is destined to be raised from the dead and live for eternity in the presence of God. Sin came into this world through Adam. It is not important whether Adam lived as the one who is described in the bible or whether Adam was a symbol of the creation of the human soul by God. A human is not as much distinguished by his or her body as by the eternal soul created by God.

'When God created human beings, he created a being which had the freedom to decide, the freedom to be for or against God. God wanted to have a challenge, and he sure found that challenge in human beings. God wanted to make a creature in his own image. That image is the eternal soul. He wanted a creature who could freely decide between good and evil; he did not want to have a pre-programmed creature who had no freedom to decide. He wanted to have a partner in the development of the world. By creating the human race, he also made the promise that in the fullness of time a redeemer would be born who would lead humanity to its place of destiny, which, of course, is heaven.'

Harry said, 'I never have heard such a short format of the history of humanity before. Don't you think you are too abstract in your reasoning? It makes sense to me, but is your statement not too controversial and against the teaching of the Christian, Jewish and Islamic religions?'

The angel answered, 'The bible was written thousands of years ago when there were only a few people who could read or write. The mysteries had to be explained in a language which everybody would understand. How could you teach these rather difficult events to people who had very little education, were mostly illiterate and had, at best, a very limited comprehension of God's plan of salvation? The best way to teach this truth is by simple examples, not through sublime trains of thought. I am not an authority on the creation of humanity. Therefore I cannot tell you the full truth of how it happened. I can only tell you that the distinction of being a human is to have an eternal soul created in the image of God. I have said it many times before, that a spark of God's spirit lives in every human.

'But we should go back to the event of the resurrection of Jesus from the dead!' continued the angel. 'You said that there were many doubters, especially today, that the event did not happen, that it was impossible that this event as described in the New Testament had ever happened. Let me tell you as an opener, there were many doubters right at the moment when it happened. The first doubters did not come from the ranks of the prosecutors but from the ranks of the apostles and the followers of Jesus.'

Harry said, 'That is true. When I read the story of the resurrection, the first thing I concluded was that the apostles did not believe, that they could not even imagine that such an event was possible and that they sounded very confused and were in fact afraid. They were so confused that each of them reported the event differently and even contradictorily.'

'Yes,' said the angel. 'The first non-believers were the apostles and followers of Jesus. They were only able to believe when their eyes were opened in the knowledge that this was the plan of God; that Jesus, in fulfillment of the scriptures which document the history of salvation, had to die and rise again.'

'How then do you really see the resurrection? Was it real? Was it spiritual? Was Jesus in fact dead, or was he still alive when his body was taken from the cross?' asked Harry.

The angel answered, 'Let me answer your third question first. Yes, Jesus was really dead. As I told you before, I was the one who ensured that he was dead by piercing him with my lance into his side. Therefore I can testify that Jesus was dead. I was also there, at the time, when his resurrection took place along with a few soldiers. We were to guard the grave, the entrance of which was secured with a heavy stone. We soldiers were put there to ensure that the body of Jesus could not be stolen by his followers. The Jews were afraid they would do this and then testify that Jesus had risen. The funny thing is that the apostles did not believe in the resurrection either, at first; their eyes were closed just like everybody else's. How could they, who did not believe, steal the body of Jesus as proof that he had risen? Is this not a contradiction?'

'Well,' said Harry, 'that may be. Still, the doubts remain that there was ever a physical resurrection of Jesus, that it was maybe a figment of the imagination, that we may have to see the resurrection in a more spiritual light, not in the light of reality.'

'Harry,' the angel said impatiently, 'I thought we had made

progress! You still doubt that the spirit is not real, that the spirit is far removed from our daily life. Let me tell you one thing; the spirit is real, the spirit is the driving force and the energy of what we achieve in reality. Spirit and reality correlate with each other. But to prove my point, yes, Jesus rose in the spirit from the dead; in other words his spirit never died, but Jesus rose also in his body from the dead.'

'How could that happen?' asked Harry. 'How could Jesus *bodily* rise from the dead and walk around, eat and drink and talk with his friends? This doesn't add up. This sure is a mystery which does not make sense to me!'

'You are just like the doubting Thomas!' exclaimed the angel. 'You just do not believe that nothing is impossible for God. Look at the latest discoveries in science. Einstein proved in his theory of relativity that under certain circumstances energy, a force which has no mass, is changed into mass or a body which you can see and feel.

'Look at the other latest scientific discoveries, discoveries the effect of which cannot be fully understood yet. These discoveries are neutrinos. When you look at the stars, you assume that the stars, galaxies and black holes make up the largest body of mass in the universe. This is apparently not the case. Neutrinos are probably the largest mass in the universe. Neutrinos are the smallest particles ever discovered. Scientist speculated about them for many years in their scientific, theoretical models, but they had not been able to see or measure them, except very recently in scientific experiments in Northern Canada. These neutrinos have the capacity to go through all the bodily masses, like electrical waves go through the air. Electrical waves are, however, energy, while neutrinos are mass.

'Why do I tell you all this?' continued the angel. 'I only tell you this to make you aware that for God nothing is impossible, whether when it comes to the creation of the universe or the bodily resurrection of Jesus. The bodily resurrection of Jesus is simply a change from one bodily mass to another, from the physical body you can see and touch to the resurrected body in a different mass component. I cannot explain all the secrets of God; I am not God; I am just an angel. But all I try to tell you is that the event of the bodily resurrection was real and that you have to have faith that this event happened.'

Harry said, 'You really make the event of the resurrection plausible and real. Such explanations should give everyone hope, hope that there is life after death, hope that there is a powerful and loving God, hope that the life to come is a life of fulfillment and happiness!'

'Congratulations, Harry!' exclaimed the angel. 'You sure give me hope too; maybe all these complex discussions which we have had will finally bear fruit. Yes, you are very right. Jesus is the first born from the dead, a sign for all people that death is overcome, that death is really a transformation to a better life, a life with a full vision of God, a life in full unity with God, a life in the loving light of God's presence.

'I believe,' the angel continued, 'that we should discuss this hope for a better life in more detail. Such a discussion will elaborate the potential not only for you, Harry, but also for everyone else.'

'That would be nice!' said Harry, smiling. 'You sure can melt the ice of even the most hardened atheist and turn him into a believer. Come to think of it, there is nothing wrong with faith; in fact, it can be a source of great happiness to believe that God the Creator loves even the most hardened atheist. With this in mind, let's talk about hope.'

Hope for Eternal Life

The angel said, 'Everyone wants to have a better life and everyone hopes to achieve it some day, atheists and believers alike, just as much as victims and victimizers, male or female – simply everyone. Anybody without hope is desperate and at the end. To live without hope is to live in hell, the eternal darkness. We really should discuss your and everybody else's desire to go to heaven, whether they know it or not.

'Do you think it is a fair statement to say that everybody desires to be happy, fulfilled and at peace with him or herself?' asked the angel.

'To each its own, but I believe that everybody strives to be happy and fulfilled; however, I must say that this is a desire which is different from person to person. What you perceive to be happiness is not my perception and vice versa,' answered Harry. 'I always thought, and now I have my doubts that lots of money stashed away in the Caribbean would make me happy. But I am changing my mind after talking with you.'

'I can assure you,' said the angel, 'that you will never find full happiness in this life, and I can vouch for that statement. You will find your fulfillment when you live in heaven which is in complete unity with Jesus the Christ, when you are engulfed in his love eternal, which can be compared to a ray of light of indescribable beauty. You simply do not have any more desires than to live in this light.'

Harry said, 'Can you describe heaven? Can you describe your experience?'

The angel answered, 'Heaven is difficult to describe because it is an experience which cannot be expressed in human language. Your soul, as we said before, has embedded in its core, a spark of God's spirit. This spark may be dormant, very small or very bright. If it is very bright, then you can call yourself a saint; if it is very small, then you have lots of room to grow into a saint; and if it is dormant, then you are not aware that God's spirit lives in you and you wind up as spiritually dried up desert cactus. I apologized for this descriptive expression before but I just could not refrain from saying so.'

Harry said with a smile, 'You are forgiven. You see I have learned a lot already. If you had compared me yesterday to this cactus, I would have called my lawyers and sued you for slander. Today I am different. I can take those small jibes. But let's get serious about the question about what heaven is like.'

The angel said, 'This is a space experience where you have life to the fullest, to your fullest potential, where you live in full community with God, where God shares freely – just like he did with Jesus the Christ – his divinity. This is a space where you have no more desires but where you simply want to be forever and hope that it never changes. You are filled to the brim; you have reached your full potential.'

'Is it difficult to get there?' asked Harry. 'I still remember the gospel in which Jesus tells his followers it is easier for a camel to go through the eye of a needle than a rich man to get to heaven. I am fairly rich, and I am not willing to part with my money that easily. I also have another question. There is this parable about the last judgment where Jesus divides humanity into goats and sheep. The sheep go to heaven and the goats go to hell. That is frightening, especially since I classify myself now as one of those goats.'

'Don't be scared!' answered the angel. 'Remember how we discussed truth? Some people have a higher knowledge of what is truth than others. It is like a treasure for which you are responsible. If you are responsible for a lot, then God will ask you for a lot. If you have less of this treasure or knowledge of the truth, then you will be asked for less. This treasure is the truth of God's spirit living in you, and Jesus said clearly, "The spirit blows where he will."'

The angel continued, 'To be a saint means to live already on earth in God's spirit to your fullest capability, even though you do not have the full vision yet.'

'You speak wisely,' said Harry, 'but still you have not answered my second question. What happens to the goats? Will they really go to hell, and how do you see the last judgment?'

The angel answered, 'Let's talk about people, rather than sheep or goats. Yes, there are people who, after spending a life living in God's spirit on earth, will go directly to heaven. They come from all walks of life; they come from all corners of the world. And then there are others who will go first to purgatory, an existence – however brief – in which they get a better vision of God's will. It is a space in which your vision is not impaired by the desires and disruptions on earth, a space where you suddenly realize the destination your soul will have to take to reach life to the fullest potential and capabilities. This may take time; the only time measurement there is in the life after death.'

'This is interesting!' Harry said. 'To me, purgatory was always related to fire, pain and suffering. How about judgment? How does that work?'

'Well,' said the angel, 'you only really judge yourself. You see, in purgatory you are faced with the full truth and with the full potential you had according to the gifts you had been given. If you did not measure up to what was expected of you, then you have to suffer. It's suffering, not in the physical sense, but more in the sense of lost potential, which means what you could have achieved but did not or were not able to do. Your deeds have to be justifiable before God, and if they are not, then you have to repent and change. I would say in purgatory it is easier than on earth. One thing you do not need, I assure you, is money!'

Harry said, 'We talked about heaven and purgatory, but you never said anything about hell. In the olden days, I had the impression that more people went to hell than to heaven, that hell was filled to the brim with lusty, fun-loving souls, while heaven was only populated by a few saints who lived a good, but essentially boring life of prayer. I will always remember the statues of saints in the churches who looked to heaven with such a holy expression that they appeared to be unreal.'

The angel said, 'These are only expressions of artists who wanted to capture the prayerful looks of a saint. I doubt very much that most of the saints were in constant prayer. They were people of real blood. Look at me! I was a soldier who ensured that Jesus died on the cross. I ridiculed Jesus – and what am I today? I am an angel, thanks to the enormous grace of God. God even forgives the worst offenders. But let's talk about hell. Hell is hard to describe. Hell is an existence of eternal restlessness and hopelessness. Remember that you judge yourself after having seen your full potential. Those who go to hell want to go there. They also judge themselves but they believe in full vision of God that their judgment is better or more just than God's. In other words they cannot see themselves as a loving participant in the community of saints. They simply do not believe in love; they believe that God's judgment is wrong and the justification of their actions is right. I do not know whether this is possible because I have great faith in the mercy of God. I also have great faith that God will make every effort to bring the lost soul back into the fold. You remember the parable of the shepherd looking for the lost sheep. This shepherd even gave his life for all the lost sheep.'

Harry asked, 'Do you say now, that hell does not exist?'

The angel said, 'Hell exists, and it is the state of eternal damnation for Lucifer and his followers. They had a clear vision of who God really is and they rebelled. But I cannot see hell as being a place populated with humans. Christ's sacrifice on the cross and his subsequent resurrection from the dead was a victory over evil, a deed of such immense value that the whole human race was saved. Remember, if you truly love, and everybody loves in his or her life, then you will live according to the plan of God, whether you know it or not, then you are part of God's kingdom. God will not waste or forsake this spark of his spirit which he implanted into every soul.'

Harry said, 'I am impressed with your arguments. You told me before that you came to see me and make me aware of the role I have to play. You told me that I had to change. Can you tell me what you mean by that?'

'I will gladly!' answered the angel. 'I guess my talk has softened you up a bit and made you more prepared for the great things I have in mind for you. What I expect from you is not really earth-shattering, but it is important. I want you to be a partner in building the kingdom of God. How about that?'

Harry was shocked. He said, 'Me, the dried up desert cactus? A partner in building the kingdom of God? I am sure you can find a saint or some other holy man or woman to build God's kingdom. Remember, I have no experience in the spiritual aspect of life; I was spiritually dead, as you so rightly implied. How can I build the kingdom of God – and what does that mean anyway?'

'Let's discuss this in more detail,' answered the angel. 'You will be surprised about the potential you can develop in yourself!'

The Call to Build the Kingdom of God

'Harry,' the angel exclaimed, 'you are called to be a builder! You are called to build the kingdom of God and have joy doing so. Are you surprised?'

Harry was speechless. This did not happen too often in his life. He always had an answer to everything and usually the last word in every discussion was his. He said, 'My friend, you have got to be kidding! You call me strange names and compare me to a desert cactus, dried up spiritually for years and here you tell me to build a kingdom. I don't even know what this means. What do you mean, the kingdom of God?'

The angel answered with a smile, 'I expected this comment from you. Shakes you up a little bit, doesn't it? Yes, I repeat, you are called to build the kingdom of God. Actually this is not too difficult at all; in fact, after we talk about it, you will quickly realize how easy it is and, I guarantee, it will be joyful. But we must do this in various steps because the kingdom of God is not a visible kingdom with a hierarchy and bureaucracy. It is a kingdom which you build within yourself, within your soul. If you really want to build this kingdom then take the first step. The first step is prayer.'

'You know what prayer is, Harry?' asked the angel.

'I have not prayed for a long while. I really have no experience in praying,' said Harry.

The angel said with an excited voice, 'Harry, you really don't know what you have missed! Prayer is to communicate with God in a very direct way. Through prayer, you will experience the joy of God's friendship within you. God is not far away; God is very close and God is in your soul. There are so many devotional prayers but the easiest way to pray is to simply ask God to be present in your daily life.'

Harry said, 'You mean, to invoke the spirit of God to be with me day in, day out? There are more than six billion people out there! Just imagine they all say the same prayer! God would have a lot of work to do with them, day in, day out!'

The angel said, 'Compare God with the source of light, a spiritual light which is brighter than the light of the sun. That light gives you the energy to sustain life as you see it. This light is the motivation to make you successful in your life. You just need to be aware that this is the power of God within you.'

Harry said, 'These are wonderful words you use! But it all sounds a little abstract and generic. Can you be more specific?'

'Of course I can!' answered the angel. 'Jesus taught a very simple prayer which encompasses all that is necessary to pray. It is short, to the point, easy to understand and you can rest assured that if someone who comes from God tells you that this is the prayer you should say, then you can expect that such a prayer is effective.'

Harry said, 'You mean, of course, the prayer, "Our father, who art in heaven..." I have not prayed that in a long time! Why don't you explain it? Or, let's reflect on it awhile.'

'Gladly!' said the angel. 'When you call God "our father", you address him as you would talk to your own father. Jesus wants you to address God like a child calling his dad. Father is the provider, the listener, the one who cares, the one who wants to do the best for you. This father, whom you address in the ultimate prayer, is the one who is present in your daily life. His name is holy, which means perfect in every way. In this prayer, you petition the father to fulfill seven wishes. The first one is to ask him to send his kingdom into your soul.'

Harry said, 'That is it? What do you mean by kingdom?'

The angel said, 'Of course it is the kingdom of love. God's kingship is based on love and on nothing else. It is a gentle and kind love; it not a tough love based on threats and authority. It is simply a love offered to you freely, like the father who, in the parable of the prodigal son, offers his lost son. Therefore you build the kingdom in yourself first and then bring the light of this love to your neighbor. You can do this in many ways: through kindness, through understanding, through smiles, through happiness, through caring, by simply being positive. There are countless ways to express love!'

The angel carried on, 'The next petitions are that God's will be done in building this kingdom here on earth, where you still have the imperfect vision of God, in the same way as God's will is being done in heaven, where there is the perfect vision of God.'

The angel continued, 'We ask God to provide us with the necessities of life. Then we ask him to forgive our failings, which he will forgive. In return he asks us to forgive our neighbors, who failed against us...'

Harry interrupted. 'Now we come to the most difficult part of the prayer, a part which I always had trouble with and could not understand. It is the part where we ask God not to lead us into temptations. How can God be a loving God if he is so devious as to lead us into temptations, in other words, lead us to the possibility of failings? How do you explain that, my friend?'

The angel answered, 'This part has been misunderstood for generations. God does not *lead* anybody into situations where he or she can be tempted to fail the command of love. This part means that we ask God not to put us to a test. It is our lack of understanding God's will and our weakness that may lead us to fail the test. Remember, Lucifer was put to a test, even though he lived in the full vision of God, and he failed this test. You know what happened to him. In this part of the prayer, we simply ask God not to test us because of the risk of failure, since we do not have a clear understanding of God's will.'

'I never thought in these terms!' said Harry. 'Your explanation makes much more sense.'

The angel continued, 'The final petition is like a cry for help. Evil is in this world; evil is sometimes hard to discover. We have seen that evil is not fully understood by the human mind despite the progress made in understanding who God is, and the progress made in understanding human dignity. And still the father of lies, the Prince of Darkness, is able to be destructive to the human race because he can make a lie seem true.'

'This is well spoken,' said Harry, and he continued, 'My friend, through these reflections I just had an inspiration, which may surprise you. I believe that this prayer, in the way you explained it, is so universal and generic that it should appeal to all major religious denominations in this world – Jewish, Christian,

Muslim, Hindu and Buddhist. Just suppose the Palestinians and Jews who fight over the right to live in Jerusalem would use this prayer every day. I could visualize a place to be built in Jerusalem where both pray for peace using this and other prayers. They would be united in spirit and suddenly experience this unity and peace in their daily lives. Then they would really fulfill the will of God. Would it not be great to have Jerusalem become a city as God intended it to be, a city of peace and love, a city dedicated to the visible kingdom of God in this world for all humanity to see? It could be a city where everyone, especially Jews, Muslims and Christians can experience the love of God in unity. I doubt that this will ever happen.'

'Harry, that is a wonderful inspiration,' said the angel, full of admiration. 'You sure surprised me with your idea. You made more progress then I thought it to be possible. Yes, the rift between the Jews and Palestinians is great. They both hate and mistrust each other, despite the fact that they pray to the same God. They are like unruly children, full of jealousy, hate and anger. God would love to see Jerusalem become a city of peace, dedicated to the whole humanity, a true symbol of God's kingdom. It can be done, but it requires love, compromise and understanding. It requires that both Jews and Palestinians pray together in unity. The prayer Jesus taught is so universal, that it may appeal to both. This may happen one of these days, maybe not in your lifetime, but for sure in God's lifetime. Remember, God is patient. God as revealed through Jesus is the God of love and peace. This love will overcome the evil of hate, war and injustice, and even will bring Jews and Palestinians together, so that they can also live in peace and harmony.'

Harry said, 'I am glad that I surprised you. You see I am willing to listen and think. In fact I find our dialogue more and more interesting. You sure have given me a lot of insight into the basic requirements of building a relationship with God, which according to your terminology, means building the kingdom of God. Is this all or are there other ways and means to build the kingdom?'

'Yes, there are!' answered the angel. 'You can enhance the kingdom very much by celebrating the Eucharist.'

Harry said, 'I have not been to mass for so many years. I strayed away because I did not see any meaning in this ceremony. I was bored and I did not understand.'

'That is too bad, you do not know what you have missed!' exclaimed the angel. 'The Eucharist is where Jesus Christ offers himself every day in the form of bread and wine to the participants as a renewal of his sacrifice on the cross. This is, of course, a matter of faith, and the understanding of what the Eucharist means and who has the authority to celebrate it is a stumbling block to the unity of the various Christian denominations. Some say it is simply a meal; others believe it signifies the body and blood of Christ, but nothing more. The Roman Catholic Church teaches that the priest through his ministry changes in a spiritual way bread and wine into the *real* body and blood of Christ. This is a matter of faith, but it is central to the Roman Catholic Church. It is the faith built on the teachings of the apostles, the first witnesses and participants of the first Eucharist on the day before the crucifixion.'

Harry said, 'I guess the opinions about the Eucharist diverge quite a bit?'

'Yes, that is true,' said the angel. 'But if you have faith in God and believe that this is the faith of the apostles, the direct witnesses, then you should also believe that the Eucharist is in the spiritual way the body and blood of Christ. By participating in the Eucharist, you re-enact the sacrifice of Christ on the cross spiritually. This act is the ultimate act of love and redemption of the world. You, Harry, by participating in this spirit in the Eucharist will become a partner with Christ in the building of God's kingdom.'

'What you say is overwhelming, and I surely cannot comprehend totally what you said. In fact most people participating in the Eucharist cannot comprehend this in its totality either!' said Harry.

After a moment of silence, Harry continued, 'You mean, if I participate in the Eucharist in the faith you just described, I can help in the redemption of the humanity? In other words I can help realize the kingdom of God not only in myself but also in others who are non-believers? That is incomprehensible!'

The angel answered, 'Harry, you man of little faith! If you had the faith of a mustard seed, you would be an important partner in God's plan for building his kingdom. The Eucharist is Jesus in the midst of the believers. Jesus is here ready to sacrifice himself again and again. He can only do this if you, the believer, participates in this sacrifice by receiving the Eucharist during mass. God shares his divinity with you and lives within you.'

Harry was shocked. 'I cannot comprehend this! Give me some time! Remember you compared me to a spiritually dried up desert cactus. It will take a while to bring this cactus back to life!'

'I will be patient,' said the angel, 'and I can wait. Remember, in eternity time is of no importance.'

The angel continued, 'I would like to make you aware of another aspect which you as a believer should realize, and that is living in the friendship of God. Let us talk about God being a your friend.'

The Joy and Trust to Live in the Friendship of God

The angel said, 'Harry, God asks you to call him a friend. Your relationship to God will be like a relationship between friends, not like the one between a master and a servant or slave. A friend listens; a friend cares; a friend shares; a friend is someone who will help. It is a real personal relationship available to you if you so wish to take advantage of it. Do you realize this?'

'Yes,' said Harry, 'I still remember the lectures from my younger days as a pupil in religious studies. We were taught that if you ask God for something you want, he will give it to you. All you have to have is faith. I remember many times I prayed for some favors, but I never received what I asked for. That makes it hard to have faith in such promises!'

The angel said, 'I am sure you are not the only one. I am sure many faithful believe that their prayers were never answered. But they never gave God a chance to act or they expected something different than what was given to them.'

The angel continued, 'You must believe in providence, that means that God will care for you and provide you with those things which are really important in his plan. These are not necessarily those things which are important in *your* plans. Both plans may differ; however, in all fairness, God's plan has precedence over your plan. Therefore it is quite possible that you never received what you wanted. But let me tell you something; you sure received what you *needed* – and much more!'

'What do you mean by that?' asked Harry.

The angel answered, 'Did you not have a good life? Did you not find the love of your life? Did you not meet me, your guardian angel? Let me tell you the truth: you need me more than those tax lawyers and accountants who want to help you hide your money in the Caribbean. You need to wake up and find out where you truly belong, namely to your family. Beatrice needs you, and so does your son Charles. You have to fulfill God's plan relative to your responsibilities towards your family. This is not an onerous plan, but a plan which will bring you true happiness, the happiness from years ago when you first met Beatrice, the happiness you had in the first few years of your marriage when you were both so young and full of hope and love. That is what God as a true friend wants you to come back to. This is God's plan.'

Harry said, astonished, 'I never knew that the almighty God, the God of the Universe, the creator of all that is seen and unseen, has taken such an interest in me. After all I am Harry, one human being out of six billion people on this earth – and here I am talking to one of his angels who tells me that my prayers have been answered! By the way, I have not prayed for the last few years; I have not even believed that there is a God who will take a personal interest in my affairs. How do you explain that?'

The angel said with a smile, 'These were not your prayers, but these were the prayers of Beatrice and especially the prayers of your son Charles. You know that he has a few difficulties, that he is not as perfect as you want him to be. You know that he may not be as smart as your other children. But God does not look at these things. God compares such a person to a flower which has not blossomed yet. But one thing Charles has, and that is his unconditional trust in God. Charles, even though he can't express his innermost thoughts the way you are able to do, prayed with such honesty, faith and trust that God had no choice but to send me to have a dialogue with you. You see, prayers are answered. It may not be your prayers, but prayers from someone who cares for you.'

Harry was really shocked now. He had never taken Charles seriously and had often treated him like a burden he had never wanted but had to put up with. Charles was for him a continuous source of arguments between Beatrice, to a point where on one occasion he said loudly to his wife in front of Charles that he never wanted Charles in the first place and that an abortion should have been the right solution for this ongoing nuisance of a son. He did not realize that Charles had understood what he had been saying.

Harry asked the angel, 'At what point did Charles pray for me and Beatrice?'

The angel answered, 'It was at the moment when you were having a particular argument and when you made a terrible comment. At that point Charles asked God for help. He may not have been able to explain all his feelings, but that is not important to God. It is not important to God whether you are intelligent, rich or a respected member of society. It is important that you have absolute trust and faith in God, and ask for his help as a friend.'

After a moment of silence the angel asked, 'Do you have some American dollars in your pocket, and do you have faith in the value of this currency?'

Harry was perplexed and said, 'Why?'

'Just give me a bill and I will show you!' answered the angel.

Harry took an American $20 bill out of his wallet and gave it to the angel. The angel took it and showed it to Harry.

'What do you see on the back side of this bill written like an emblem over the White House?' asked the angel.

Harry said, 'In God we trust.'

The angel said, 'To my knowledge there is no other currency in this world issued by a government with the imprint "In God we trust". The American people, whether believers or not, put as a community their trust in God. I always wondered whether a true and convinced atheist would use an American dollar bill, being fully aware of the fact that this bill of exchange expresses trust not only in the value of the currency but also in God. Did you ever think about that?' asked the angel.

Harry said, 'That thought never even occurred to me! But you are right; as a true and convinced atheist, I should not handle that currency.

'On second thought,' Harry continued with a smile, 'my reason for being an atheist has changed since I met you. Therefore I am not concerned about using American money. It is one of the strongest currencies at present and I can surely see its value.'

The angel said, 'I knew you would come around to my way of thinking. But let's carry on with our train of thought. When you have trust in God, whom you may call your friend, what kind of feelings will that create in you? Will you be happy? Will you be joyful or will you be scared of the responsibility you have to carry? You must realize that you will be consciously aware of the presence of God in your life. What kind of feeling will that create in you?'

Harry said, 'Boy, that is a difficult question to answer. After all, I am only one person under so many and I was never really consciously aware of the fact that the spirit of God lives in my soul. But if I have faith and trust in God's friendship with me, then I can see myself being re-energized; I can see myself happy; I can see myself full of joy and hope. I can see myself as a lover who wants to spread this wonderful feeling of joy to all the others.'

'Well spoken, my friend!' said the angel. 'You see, I don't even need to call you a dried up desert cactus anymore; instead I will call you a friend who has the potential to move mountains, mountains which block the clear view of what is important and what is not important in your life.

'Harry,' the angel continued, 'we are almost at the end of our dialogue. We have covered the spirit of truth and love, faith in God's love, the desire to have life to the fullest in heaven, the call to build God's kingdom and the joy of doing so. I would like to cover two more points which I consider important. I would like to discuss with you wisdom. I would like you to be aware of the fact that you have to search for wisdom, for God's wisdom. God's wisdom will lead you to do what is right in the eyes of God. Would you mind if we discuss what is understood under God's wisdom?'

Harry said, 'You know I was very skeptical in the beginning but you were able to change my mind. I was shocked when you told me about the prayers of my son Charles, and I feel very sorry that I ever made that comment.'

Harry continued, 'My friend – I hope I can call you a friend – I look forward to discussing wisdom with you. I am very sure that I will need all the wisdom in the world to make the right decisions when I go home and face my family. In fact, I will ask God to give me the wisdom of Solomon to find the right words when I talk to Charles and Beatrice.'

The angel said, 'You do not need the wisdom of Solomon! You need God's wisdom as help. I am sure that if you ask God, he will be very willing to help you. After all he is keenly interested in seeing that the prayers of Beatrice and Charles are answered.'

The Wisdom to Know God's Will

The angel said, 'When you think of wisdom, you probably think of an old man, sitting in silence, in a forest alone by himself deep in thought. Am I right Harry?'

Harry nodded and said, 'I guess so. I don't really know what wisdom is or how to describe it. I only know that when you make decisions based on wisdom, you will never be wrong. A wise man will always come up with a balanced view when making a decision, taking all the pros and cons into consideration. Am I right?'

'Just about!' answered the angel. 'The only missing component of a wise decision is that the decision is inspired by God. God is the ultimate source of wisdom; in fact, in the Old Testament wisdom was always compared to God. You probably know that wisdom is feminine in most languages. It is the feminine side of God.'

'If that is the case,' said Harry impatiently, 'then why are so many decisions wrong, despite the fact that they are made by so many so-called wise old men?'

'In order to make a wise decision, you need time to think, time to pray, time to meditate. The power of meditation is enormous. In meditation you simply step back from your daily life and you take a rest.'

The angel stopped for a moment and then continued, 'You see the nature surrounding us here, the sun, the mountains, the ocean, all these invite us to meditation. It is wise to step back, enjoy and listen to God's word in your soul. God speaks quietly. God cannot be understood if you constantly surround yourself with a lot of noise, such as loud music or the rough and tumble of business. You need time for yourself to listen to God's word in you and to get to know his wisdom. His wisdom will guide you to what is best for you.'

Harry said, 'You've lost me! You tell me now that I should

give up all the things I like to do, such as going to a good party, living in the excitement of the business world, and live like a hermit somewhere in the woods. If you ask me to give all these things up for the sake of wisdom and God's word in my heart, then I have to disappoint you. I am unwilling to do so because I happen to enjoy them. And by the way I happen to be a realist; I have to live up to the demands of a certain lifestyle, which is expensive. I doubt that it would be wise to give up all these things which I enjoy.'

'Don't get too upset with me!' said the angel with an ironic smile. 'You don't have to give up anything. You can carry on with your lifestyle. God would not dare ask you for a great sacrifice. All I try to do is to make you aware of the great opportunity you may want to utilize when you take a moment's rest for meditation. It will be a moment when you ask yourself what God wants from you. A time set aside for meditation is never lost. It helps you to regain your strength and rejuvenates you. It also gives God time so that his words can take root in your soul.'

Harry said, 'You sure make me think! I was never really fond of meditation. I always was a man of action. But you are right! The many wrong decisions I made could have been avoided if I had only been a little bit more patient. I guess with meditation you get a more balanced view upon which you can make a wiser decision.'

'Yes, you are right!' said the angel. 'I also still have to learn to be more patient, especially with a man whom I compared to a dried up desert cactus. You see, even angels have room for improvement.'

After a brief moment the angel continued, 'Harry, I want to conclude our discussion. I was sent to answer the prayers of a child who deeply loves you. My mission is to help you to make a decision. I cannot make that decision for you. All I can do is make you aware of God's will. Through our dialogue I hope I gave you a glimpse of what is important in your life. I hope I made you aware of the fact that God can be your best friend. He is not the authoritarian father figure you always thought he should be, a God far removed from your daily life. We proved that a spark of his divine spirit lives in you as in every other human being. God wants you to be guided to make the right decision, and I was called to be your guide. I want to discuss with you now the decision you have to make, whether to go to your meeting with your tax lawyer and accountants or whether to listen to a child who needs your help and love.'

The angel continued, 'I believe we are now at the moment where you have to make the right choice. In order to do that we need some time to rest and meditate to find out what God wants you to do.'

The Wisdom to Do God's Will

Harry and the angel sat on the bench quietly, each occupied with his own thoughts. Harry suddenly felt a wonderful feeling of love and warmth overcoming him, a feeling which he had not experienced for many years. This warmth came from deep inside his body, like a new source of energy and power. It was a beautiful feeling of such indescribable tenderness. He felt the desire to hurry home and hug and kiss Beatrice and especially his son Charles.

Harry said to the angel, 'I don't think that we have to discuss in great detail what God wants from me now. In this short moment of meditation, I suddenly realized my failings but also felt the enormous power of love. It is like a new source of energy coming from inside of my body. I suddenly feel free, the freedom of someone who has carried a great burden in his soul for a long time even though he didn't realize it. This burden is the wall which I have built around me, which nobody was able to penetrate, not even Beatrice or Charles or my other children.'

Harry continued, 'I was so involved in my business affairs that I neither had the desire to communicate with my wife, nor the desire to pay much attention to my children. I honestly believe that I am the source of the unhappiness in my family. I always blamed it on everyone else. All of them tried to reach out to me, but I refused to let them come close to me. I never attempted a real communication, talking about what was really important, listening to what they had to say, touching when a hug or handshake was needed, smiling when a smile of encouragement was required. I was only critical and cold.'

He stopped for a while, but the angel encouraged him to carry on.

Harry said, 'You know, I always blamed the lack of warmth and the lack of real communication on all the others but myself. How could they develop a real closeness to me when I rejected every approach? The wall which I believed Beatrice had built around herself and Charles is really the reflection of the wall I had created in the first place. I was the one who started it first. I did not want anybody, especially any member of my family, to penetrate the security of this wall. I felt secure but really I was not; I felt a sense of freedom within the borders of this wall, but this freedom was false. It was more an encampment and constraint then real freedom; I felt strong and invincible, but my strength was built on weakness. I thought I was happy but this happiness was the pretense that satisfaction comes from greed to achieve great wealth at all costs.'

Harry stopped. The angel had listened patiently to Harry's confession. He realized that the first step to renewal was the acknowledgment of the wrongs done in the past.

He said to Harry, 'What you said was beautiful. It was like the prayer you always wanted to say but never could express. You are like your son Charles. He may be slow in learning and slow in school, but Charles has the capacity to express what is really important, namely absolute trust in God. He cannot express what is in his soul in words but he can express it with the look in his eyes. Harry, please turn back home and reach out to Beatrice, Charles and your twins. The burden which you so clearly identified in your confession will be lifted. You will be free; you will realize a new source of energy, an energy you never thought you had. You will love and you will be loved. That is the will of God. You may think that I, an angel sent by God, am a miracle. Let me tell you, there are angels in your daily life which are much closer to you than I ever will be. Maybe Beatrice is an angel; maybe Charles is one; maybe the people you meet are angels. You do not have to look far. How do you think I obtained this motorcycle?'

Harry said, 'That is a question I always wanted to ask you. How did you do it, and how did you learn how to drive it?'

'Well,' said the angel, 'God even has friends among the Hell's Angels. They sometimes don't realize that they can be real angels. The goodness which is in everyone comes from God, the goodness in caring for others, the goodness of making someone smile, all these things come from God. You just have to make the connection.'

Harry said, 'If there is hope for the Hell's Angels, then there is even hope for me, I guess.'

'Of course there is!' said the angel. 'I have great hope and great faith in you, that you make the decision which will result in real happiness and true freedom. I do not have to tell you what this decision should be. You will know it best yourself.

'Harry,' the angel continued, 'it is time that we say good-bye. You have work to do, and so do I.' He continued with a shy smile in his eyes, 'Can you help me with this motorcycle? I am really not used to driving this machine. I still think I am driving a chariot with two horses.'

Harry said, 'No problem. That is the least I can do for you.'

Harry and the angel picked up the motorcycle and Harry held it straight so that the angel could mount it easily. With great difficulty the angel started the machine, put it in first gear and headed toward the road north to Whistler. The angel waved with one of his hands and disappeared around the next corner.

Harry and Beatrice, their Marriage Renewed

The sun was still shining low over the mountainous islands to the west, lying low like a great yellow and orange ball. Its rays penetrated through the scattered clouds pointing like fingers to the earth.

Harry was still sitting on the bench, deep in thought. Did he really meet an angel or was it just a dream? He heard the traffic roaring by and reality sank in. He said to himself, 'I must have been crazy to think that an angel would visit me and talk about God and what is important in life. Who am I to believe in such miracles? I am a man of reason who has no time for those esoteric spiritual thoughts of what is truth and what in life has real value. I am a businessman who must go on and create wealth and earn money for himself.'

Harry looked at his watch. 'You see,' he said to himself, 'it is still about 5 P.M. But why am I sitting on this bench? I was supposed to be driving to Whistler to meet with the tax lawyers.'

He suddenly remembered the reason for being here at the lookout. It was, of course, the blowout of his front tire. He remembered vividly the incident with that crazy motorcycle driver, the one he almost killed. He remembered also that this man had stopped and introduced himself as an angel, not as a Hell's Angel but as a Heaven's Angel. So it must have been true that he had this dialogue...or was it? He recalled the many subjects they had discussed, but he could not understand how it could still be about 5 P.M. If it was, the discussion could not possibly have taken place. After all, they must have talked for at least a few hours. He looked again in astonishment at his watch and recalled the comment the angel had made, that in eternity time is of no importance. Did he really get a glimpse of eternity, or was it just a hallucination? He could not come to a conclusion and decided to go back to his car and check the tire which had to be fixed.

There on the front tire, written just like the identification of the tire manufacturer, were the following words: *Greetings from your guardian angel.* Harry looked again and yes, these few words were clearly visible on the outside of the tire, not written with a crayon, but imprinted just like the name of the tire manufacturer, like a constant reminder which could only be eradicated if the tire was changed. As long as he drove the car using this specific tire, Harry would be reminded of the dialogue he had had with the angel.

Now a few of the points which they so intensely had discussed came back culminating in the statement that it would be wise to do God's will, the will of a God who is best described as a God of love whose spirit lives in all of us. All there was to do was to recognize this divine spirit and be more aware of its presence.

Harry felt suddenly the same warmth in his body which he had experienced when they had discussed the wisdom to recognize God's will. He remembered now the words an old professor from his days in the university had spoken. He had said, 'Love and do as you please. True freedom is to do the will of God.'

Harry opened the door to his car, started the engine and slowly moved to approach the road. He still was deep in thought and suddenly he remembered Beatrice and his son Charles. He recalled the wonderful days of his early marriage, the birth of the twins and also the birth of Charles. How could he resent Charles if even God would answer his prayers? How could he neglect Charles, who had shown great love despite the fact that he, his father, had always thought him to be a nuisance? Even though he had been mistreated and mentally abused by his father, Charles had shown a great love for him.

Harry felt the same warmth as he had experienced when the angel was present. He said to himself, 'I must go back to my family. I do love them all very much; I simply cannot destroy what is dear to me.' He wheeled the car around so that the tires screeched. He thought that the angel would be relieved when he heard this screech as a sign that Harry was going back to where he belonged.

Impatiently he raced the engine and the car sped towards

Vancouver. At one of the exits close to his home, he turned off the highway and stopped in a little flower shop. Initially he wanted to buy fifty red roses for Beatrice; then he thought that it would appear as fake. While in the flower shop, the comment about a spiritually dried up desert cactus came to his mind… He said to himself, 'It would be a wonderful reminder of the dialogue I had with the angel if I bought this cactus. Maybe Beatrice will not understand, but I will, and whenever I build a wall around myself, whenever I am Harry the pompous fool, I will look at this cactus and say, 'Hey little plant, teach me a lesson.'

Harry purchased a small cactus with a few blue blossoms. He ran back to the car full of excitement as he approached his home. When he opened the door, he saw Beatrice with Charles sitting on the table, both deeply involved solving some mathematical problem for school. Beatrice was as usual very patient, while Charles was trying diligently to write down some numbers in a schoolbook.

When Harry opened the door, they both looked up. They saw Harry excited like they had never seen him before. The dull and miserable expression on his face was gone. His eyes sparkled like they had never before. He took Beatrice's hand and pressed it to his heart. He also took Charles' hand and cried out, 'Beatrice and Charles, get up fast! I want to hug and kiss both of you!'

The surprise in both of their eyes could not be overlooked. They had never seen Harry so emotional and spontaneous. Every move or every word was always calculated and well thought out. And here he was, full of smiles and happiness.

He said to both, 'Beatrice and Charles, I want to kiss and hug you. I want to start a new life. Yes, I was distant and cold, but I will change! Yes, I neglected you, my family, because of all kinds of reason, but I will change!'

'Beatrice, I love you very much!' he exclaimed, 'I have not treated you very well in the past few months and our relationship was on the breaking point. My excuses were always based on reasons which were really not relevant. Beatrice, I want to change and I hope that you can forgive me. I really want you to be happy, as happy as we both were when we first started out in the adventure of our marriage. I want to do all the things we both promised ourselves we would do.'

Beatrice could not believe her eyes and ears. Was Harry real? She had never seen her husband so full of excitement, but when he took her in his arms, she felt the warmth of his body. Suddenly she also felt the same warmth coming from the depth of her body. She said, 'Harry, I love you too. I have not said these words for so many weeks and months. They almost sound strange, but Harry, we both have to start again. Love is wonderful, and many times I suffered – but I did not know why. I also was cold, had built a wall around myself not to be penetrated by anyone except our son Charles. He was my security for all these months and weeks when we could not find a common ground, when we could not jump over these walls which we had built. Harry, let's not build these walls again.'

Harry said with a smile, 'Every time I become the pompous old Harry, look at this cactus which I bought as a present. There is a story attached to this cactus, which I will tell you one of those days. Just have faith in my love for you and for all the children. Let us rejoice and be glad and celebrate.'

Harry turned to Charles. Charles had watched in silence as his parents kissed and hugged, and he looked up with his deep silent eyes. He said a prayer of thanks, not in words but in the expression of his face, a face which showed such a deep understanding, an understanding which was deeper than his parents would ever realize.

Harry said to Charles, 'Son, I am very proud of you. For me you will be "Charles the Great". You are the one who brought me back to life and made me aware of what really is the "ultimate" in this life. These are not things I treasured. The ultimate gift in this life is love, the gift you share with both of your parents so freely. Just look at this little cactus which I brought home. This cactus will blossom in the years to come and so will you. Your smiles will make people happy. I am glad you are my son, and I am glad that you are alive and well.'

Charles was speechless. He could not comprehend all the things his father had just told him, but he saw the blossoms on the little cactus and he smiled, a shy and innocent smile, but a smile full of love.

And so there was a cactus in the desert of Nevada. This cactus was dried up and almost dead for years. Through a miracle this dried up desert cactus started to bloom. It had magnificent blossoms. People would stop often when passing by and admire the beauty of this plant. And even the angel glanced from heaven at this cactus. While he admired the blossoms, a smile brightened up his face and he said to himself, full of satisfaction, 'A job well done.'

Printed in the United Kingdom
by Lightning Source UK Ltd.
100987UKS00001BB/9